The Desolate

The Desolate

Everything, Volume Three

STEVEN DeLAY

RESOURCE *Publications* · Eugene, Oregon

THE DESOLATE
Everything, Volume Three

Resource Publications
An Imprint of Wipf and Stock Publishers
199 W. 8th Ave., Suite 3
Eugene, OR 97401

www.wipfandstock.com

PAPERBACK ISBN: 978-1-6667-4015-8
HARDCOVER ISBN: 978-1-6667-4016-5
EBOOK ISBN: 978-1-6667-4017-2

APRIL 25, 2022 12:07 PM

As always,
to Gabriella

ONE

T HE words were plain. It wasn't at all a question of whether one understood them or not. It was simply a matter of whether one trusted them.

Blessed is the man that walketh not in the counsel of the ungodly, nor standeth in the way of sinners, nor sitteth in the seat of the scornful.

But his delight is in the law of the Lord; and in his law doth he meditate day and night.

And he shall be like a tree planted by the rivers of water, that bringeth forth his fruit in his season; his leaf also shall not wither; and whatsoever he doeth shall prosper.

The ungodly are not so, but are like the chaff which the wind driveth away.

Therefore the ungodly shall not stand in the judgment, nor sinners in the congregation of the righteous.

For the Lord knoweth the way of the righteous, but the way of the ungodly shall perish.

This was the profoundness of Scripture. Its truth was not relegated only to the proposition or the judgment. In that respect, the truth was not a matter of mere belief. The truth was something one did, which was why the truth of the deeds was outwardly manifest. But the truth was also in the heart, which only God saw. Consequently, the realm of everyday opinion, of empty speech, of lazy judgment, of lies and half-truths, was subverted in the name of true deeds, and true thoughts.

Understandably, the world's institutions and systems, and those who relished partaking in them, would hate such a truth, because it exposed their form of preferred truth for the mere semblance it was. As for the words he had just read in the Psalms, they were not merely words on a page. They were living words, words that explicated essential laws structuring the nature of reality and governing human life, words that were sure to guide one properly, if one understood and obeyed.

He laughed to himself. Of course, anyone looking at him sitting here in this living room would think his own life was a powerful example of why not to obey these words. After all, he had lost his life, or had it taken from him. To begin with, his academic career was essentially over. Having been defamed, mocked, and ridiculed in Oxford, he was now abandoned by many longtime friends and family. Alison partly resented him for having put them in the situation in which they now found themselves. For one thing, it was unlikely they would be able to start a family of their own anytime soon. For another, those who had brought him to this point had no intention of ceasing. They appeared to have him where they wanted, and they would only press their advantage. He knew the story they were circulating about him, since he knew how they thought, which made it easy to anticipate their lies.

According to them, he was a disgraced, disgruntled, paranoid graduate student, who had washed out of Oxford after not hacking it, and who was living on the fringes of society, believing himself to be the victim of a satanic conspiracy meant to destroy his work and reputation. Of course, there was in fact a cabal of powerful people doing this to him. But that didn't matter. Being right didn't count for anything in the world, since the world itself was a lie. If anything, being right was a liability to one's social existence.

Those plotting against him knew most people wouldn't understand, or care, what was really going on, and if there were any others who did happen to understand and care, there was nothing they would be able to do about it. He sighed, opened the apartment door, and took a seat at the chair. The man from downstairs, Trevor, was in the vegetable garden working on the tomatoes. The man waved.

"Hey, neighbor! How's it going?"

"Good. How are you?"

"Just enjoying another beautiful day," Trevor said. The man's dog ran into the garden, barking at the butterflies.

The man collected his tools, and looked up.

"If you and Alison ever want any tomatoes, let me know."

"Thank you," he said.

He thought about what everyone he knew in Oxford would be doing at the moment. Right about now, the philosophers would be in the Strawson Room. The theologians would be at Evensong before one of their dinners. He laughed softly. The esteem of men was nothing compared to the honor that came from God alone. Those he knew would scoff if he ever said that. In fact, his old friends and most of his extended family believed that was the very sort of preposterous thinking responsible for the self-inflicted misfortune that had befallen him in Oxford.

After moving out of Linda and Stuart's into the apartment, he had contacted his groomsmen back in California, attempting to explain what had happened in Oxford. But after having already read the article about him online and having heard that his first viva had been flunked, they weren't listening. They'd already made up their minds. It didn't matter that the viva was voided for being irregular. And it didn't matter that he had exonerating evidence showing that the things said about him in the newspaper had been lies. The gossip had already taken his old friends in. In a way, then, they'd made up their minds in light of what they'd wanted to see. They had been looking for an excuse to justify their opinion of him, and the drama in Oxford provided the needed rationale. Linda and Stuart, like his friends, had known this, and used it to their own advantage. He could not prove it yet, but he assumed May, one of Alison's bridesmaids, who herself was from Texas and still kept in touch with Linda, had told Eric whatever Linda had told May. Eric had in turn told Andy, and Andy had in turn told Bert. Now that he appeared to be down and out, the jealousy and envy that had been there for years on the part of Andy and Bert was coming out. With things having gone off the rails for him at Oxford, Bert's PhD at Claremont was no longer dwarfed. The fact that Andy had become a corporate sell-out with an office job in New York City was now by comparison a prudent and respectable move. In short, his apparent failure at Oxford had made them all feel better about themselves.

Yesterday, in fact, he had received a letter from his old friends, stating that they didn't want him to share his faith with them anymore. They wanted to be friends still, the letter said, but on the condition that he respected their wishes. Of course, this was really just an ultimatum that he bracket what he stood for. At any rate, it eliminated any possibility of a genuine understanding between them. How was he supposed to share with them anything at all about his life in a friendship, if he couldn't mention his faith? The entire reason he was sitting defamed out in Texas, rather than sitting in the Strawson Room in Oxford, had been his faith.

He wanted a cigarette. If he smoked one, though, he knew it would not be only one. He reminded himself that a temptation didn't mean anything. It was merely a temptation. Just because there was a desire for something didn't mean it had to be indulged. That, he thought, was how lust deceived those it did. People made the mistake of thinking that a fleeting desire was a revelation, or a fate, something it would be dishonest to deny and not indulge. They never bothered to find out what would happen if they resisted. Thus, they succumbed continually, plunging deeper and deeper into their lusts, until the very idea of taking any critical distance from their desires became unthinkable. Desires were their chains. The bondage of sin, he thought. The craving for a cigarette passed.

It made sense that his childhood friends must see things the way they currently did. Spiritual things are foolish to those who did not yet themselves know God. Not only did it blind people to what they might otherwise see. It also made them easily manipulable. Advertisers and other propagandists knew this. The same principles of persuasion that worked on a mass level in entertainment and marketing, also could be used on a smaller scale. It was basic psychological warfare techniques. The NKVD and Stasi had used these techniques to great effect in the past. And intelligence services, private security, surveillance companies, and others use them now. Isolate the target. Publicly discredit him. Financially cripple him. Intimidate others into not wanting to help, since they're given to understand they will be targeted next if they do. At that point, people's self-interest would do the rest.

He stood up to grab his wallet from the kitchen counter inside. An afternoon walk sounded nice. For now, there was nothing more to be done about his situation other than to continue work on the book. A date for the new viva had been set, but that was a couple months away. If the network was in the meanwhile busy painting him as the Unabomber type, he was resigned to it. It was all lies, anyway. And, frankly, they weren't denying him anything he still desired. He had seen the successful academic life people strove to attain, and he had rejected it. He was content with what others considered nothing, since what they prized was nothing to him anymore. People might think finding himself where he was constituted an embarrassing fall, but he did not see it that way. He'd rather be here at his apartment working on his book than in the Strawson Room play acting with Quiller and Klaus. Right about now, they'd all be sitting down for dinner at Quod. It was a relief not to be there.

The next day, after Alison had again left for work, intellectual duty called him to Paris. Not physically, of course. He would be sitting right here at his desk. It was his attention that was called to the City of Lights, to the philosophical milieu responsible for having produced a number of the French texts he had to read, in order to get started on writing his own book. Chief among them was Levinas's *Totality and Infinity*. He picked up his copy of Levinas and was about to open to page one, when he glanced outside, and saw a hummingbird hovering outside the window. He opened the glass, and watched it through the screen. The windchimes from the neighbor's yard were tinkling, and there was a faint rainbow visible above the lawn from the water spraying out of the yard sprinkler. He set the Levinas down and surveyed his book shelf.

It has been years since he'd last read the mystics. There were volumes from Eckhart, Ruusbroec, and Avila. But he reached for his copy of Merton which felt timely. Today, the trees were speaking, but he had known long stretches where they hadn't. Hearing how Merton sustained himself during the dry spells might be edifying for later. He began flipping through the Merton, but his attention strained and then waned, as his thought was drawn to consider the nature of animals. Saint Assisi, if he recalled correctly, had been famous for thinking that the animals could instruct us in the ways of grace. Modern biology understood animals strictly in terms of their species being. But there was something fundamentally impoverished about such a view. Each animal had its own unique personality, it seemed to him. The Greeks understood this to an extent, since for them, at least for Aristotle, every living being had a soul. It was man who had a rational soul, distinguishing him from the other animals. There was a certain tendency today to accentuate the difference between animals and humans falsely. That was evident, for example, in the cruelty of animal testing by big pharma, or factory farming. At the same time, there was an opposing tendency to accentuate the commonality between animals and humans falsely. That was evident, for example, in the scientism that saw everything as being merely the result of Darwinian evolution. It was the Bible that spoke of animals and humans as in some sense equivalent, insofar as they were creatures of God. And yet, the uniqueness of humanity was preserved without either deprecating or overinflating the value of the animals. It was this deep kinship between the animals and humans that someone like the Seraphic Friar had seen so well. Animals lacked language, and, as someone like Heidegger would note, they were "poor in world," but they were nevertheless highly attuned to humans in certain ways, in a way, at least, that made them responsive to human emotions. If creation itself were God's cathedral, the animals themselves were icons of God.

He stood up from his desk and sat down on the couch to pet his cat. The cat lifted up his head gratefully, purring with delight. The gentle creature stood up and did his customary circles, rubbing its head up against his hand. "Good boy, Myshkie," he said. Myshkie was the cat's nickname. They'd named him Prince Myshkin. He had been a stray born blind in one eye. His memory turned to when they found him at the shelter, shortly before he had left for Oxford. The other cats had been shy, but Myshkin had run up to him immediately, clawing at his knees for attention. Alison had known Myshkin was his favorite.

She pointed to a generic brown cat. "What about this one? She's cute." Alison went up to pet it.

"That's Chocolate," the female worker had said.

He looked at Myshkin, "What about this one?"

"The cyclops one?" the worker said good-naturedly.

"Yeah."

"That," the worker said, picking him up in her arms, "is Moe. And those two over there are his siblings, Larry and Curley. He's the ring-leader," she said smiling.

He looked at Alison.

"You don't like him?"

"No, I like him. He has a lot of character." She paused for a moment. "I knew he would be your favorite the second we walked in here."

He laughed. "Well, of course. Look at him."

She sighed playfully, "Fine, if you want the weird one, let's get him."

"I can't leave him here! Nobody's going to take him. His eye will scare all the kids, so parents won't want him. He'll be here forever."

Here on the couch, Myshkin crawled onto his lap, and curled up into a ball, where he was soon purring in his sleep. Assisi had been correct, he thought, to think that the animals could be spiritual friends. They could bring comfort. That was noble. And their simplicity, it seemed, was an example, a humbling reminder that the animals were what they were, just as humans should be what they were. The only way for a man truly to be himself was to be in Christ. The animals, then, were a constant reminder of the God who had brought them into being, and they were calling men to him through them. His reverie was interrupted by another meow. The other cat, a female named Umi, had leapt up onto the couch, waiting for a pet. Unlike the disheveled and blind stray Myshkin, Umi was a beautiful, regal half-Bengal. Her big green eyes were always searching, and beneath her surface aloofness was a deep sensitivity. To be sure, the two made a very odd couple, but they loved each other. Umi licked Myshkin's fur, as Myshkin stood up to lick her also. He patted them both on the head, then stood up from the couch, and left them to cleaning each other.

At the desk, he considered sketching an outline for the Levinas chapter. But he was restless. He would leave it for tonight. The remaining daylight would be better spent out on a walk, he decided. A drive would be nicer, but they only had one car which Alison had taken to work. Consequently, he was stranded in a city that was notoriously unwalkable. Thankfully, the immediate neighborhood was a fairly self-sufficient oasis that provided most of the things he needed. It was a short walk to a coffee shop in one direction, in the other direction was the edge of Midtown, and the university was a twenty-minute walk.

His mind turned to campus. He really had no desire to see any of his old colleagues there, since he knew they would have heard about what had happened in Oxford. Or, more precisely, they would think they knew what had happened, though they really had no idea. What they would know was to ignore him, since it had been made clear that he was to be a professional pariah. If anybody there learned he was back and reached out to him, he would be happy to meet. But he was not going to invest effort into trying to reestablish relationships with those who weren't interested. If he ever went to campus, it would only be to use the library. Stuart, of course, would also be on campus, but because he knew that Stuart had no intention of ever discussing what had happened in Oxford, there was no reason to visit him. The same was also true of Carrell who had gone silent.

After the Proctors' decision to void the first viva, he'd sent an email to Carrell saying he'd returned to Texas. Carrell had responded, saying he'd be happy to chat with him in person after he'd sat for the new viva in a couple months. In Carrell's note, there was a notable omission. Carrell hadn't acknowledged the fact that he'd been wrong to say the academic appeal was unlikely to have succeeded. Now that the appeal had succeeded, naturally Carrell was unsure of what to do. Carrell was shrewd. Carrell would surely see that Oxford was going to have to confer the DPhil. That meant Carrell would also understand that Quiller and Klaus would simply regroup, by attempting to block the Routledge book as they had tried to block the thesis. The natural course of action for Carrell, then, was to pretend he was happy that the appeal had succeeded, while knowing that the DPhil wouldn't alter things substantially anyway. Carrell knew that he would still be blackballed. He thought about David's old comment about

Carrell wanting disciples. Having met Maureen in Oxford, it was clear David had been right about that. Maureen was a disciple, and he was not. He sighed. Even assuming Maureen had ever truly been sincere about inviting him to co-edit the volume on Carrell's work, Carrell would by now have told her to cut him from the project. If there were any intention to have him involved, after all, it would have been natural for Carrell to mention it. Carrell, however, hadn't said a word of it, and neither had Maureen, who'd simply vanished. In any case, until the viva was over, there was no point in contacting his old supervisor.

Outside, he walked down the street until he reached a narrow dirt service lane that ran between Garrott and Roseland. He thought about how all the people in the apartment complexes and houses around him had no idea about any of this. They would have of course heard of Oxford, and some might be impressed, but it wasn't something immediate to them. Of those who might care about Oxford enough to care that he was a student there, even fewer would understand the oddity of his being here in Texas. If they asked what he studied, some might be intrigued when they heard he studied philosophy, but very few people would be aware of the philosophical tradition in which he worked. Some may have heard the name of Sartre, but that would be about it. He saw how Oxford itself was a bubble. The people there came to forget that the outside world didn't care, that there was so much more to life than academic politics and accolades. He liked the perspective that the isolation here provided. By distilling everything down to the work itself, his life had been simplified. The possibility of getting drawn into thinking that all the trappings of academic success and prestige mattered had been eliminated. Out here in the neighborhood, nobody knew him, nobody knew what he was writing, and nobody would care.

Naturally, there was the worry that perhaps the work itself he was doing didn't matter. Others were more than happy to indicate that's how they viewed it. And it was a possibility he had entertained himself. He was resolved to be as honest as he could about that. If he ever came to feel that writing the book wasn't worth it, he would walk away. He was resigned to the fact that publishing it wouldn't change his material situation. No academic job was waiting. No money was waiting. No fancy title was waiting. The reward would be the book itself, and knowing that whoever might read it might gain something from reading it. If he felt like what he was writing wouldn't be worth reading, he would set it aside. He knew others wanted him to believe it was selfish and arrogant of him to continue working on an academic book, given his professional situation. If publishing it wasn't going to lead anywhere, why publish it? The practical course, from their perspective, was not to bother writing it at all, and simply to go get a job doing something else entirely. He was aware of the criticism. His mother had already been intimating that once he had the DPhil, he should turn to other things. Not doing so would be immature and selfish of him. Linda and Stuart were slightly more subtle, but the implication of their behavior was the same. By never talking about his academic future with Alison and him, they were suggesting that it was time for him to forget about it. And forgetting about it meant no longer pretending the book he was writing mattered. Over time, the lack of support he was receiving would weigh on Alison. By ignoring his work like it didn't matter, they would make her feel like she was unfairly being made to indulge him as he wasted his time on nothing, while she went off to work and the "real world." In order to neutralize this line of criticism she was sure to get about him while he was working on the book, he would find a part-time job doing something else at the same time. He wasn't yet sure what he'd do, but he'd find something.

As he walked alone, he thought about how in the past, when he had lived here in Texas the last time, on an afternoon like this, he'd have gone to the bar. He had no desire to do that now. Still, he understood why people did. Why he used to. It was the restlessness. He still got bored, and sometimes even restless, but it wasn't the same sort of restlessness. He wouldn't be able to explain the difference to anyone who might ask, but the difference was apparent to him. At the bars had been the girls. He used to regularly hear he was dreamy. He thought back to all the times the girls would say he could be a movie star, or that he looked like some actor they loved. Jude Law, Adam Brody, and Dane DeHaan. He had heard it all. He remembered the one time a girl had told him he looked like an actor, and after asking her which one, she had said none of them. "You're you. If you were an actor, girls would tell the guys they met that they looked like you." Thinking about it now, he realized they had thought he was dreamy because he was haunted. They found it deep and mysterious, even if it was ultimately an abyss within him. Once, a guy whom he later learned happened to be Justice's younger brother had told Alison he reminded him of a ghost. He wanted to be a ghost again, not in the sense of being melancholic or haunted, but wholesomely ephemeral, rendered as if nothing by a humility that left him translucent. He knew he was not nearly as conceited as he had used to be, but there was room for further purification. If, for instance, he was to be disfigured in a car crash and badly burned, he would be self-conscious to be seen in public. That was residual vanity, he thought.

He had been so immersed in reflection that he'd failed to notice he'd walked home. Standing in the lot, he looked through the wrought iron fence into the garden, then up to the door of their corner apartment on the second floor. When he got upstairs, he would sit in his chair and watch the butterflies down in the garden. "Holy Spirit, be with me. Holy Spirit, lift me up. Holy Spirit, let me hear you. Speak to me, O God. Let me not be empty. Fill me," he whispered.

At his chair, he opened to a random page in the Psalms.

> *Blessed is he that considereth the poor: the Lord will deliver him in time of trouble.*
>
> *The Lord will preserve him, and keep him alive; and he shall be blessed upon the earth: and thou wilt not deliver him unto the will of his enemies.*
>
> *Mine enemies speak evil of me, When shall he die, and his name perish?*
>
> *And if he come to see me, he speaketh vanity: his heart gathereth iniquity to itself; when he goeth abroad, he telleth it.*
>
> *All that hate me whisper together against me: against me do they devise my hurt.*
>
> *Yea, mine own familiar friend, in whom I trusted, which did eat of my bread, hath lifted up his heel against me.*
>
> *But thou, O Lord, be merciful unto me, and raise me up, that I may requite them.*
>
> *By this I know that thou favourest me, because mine enemy doth not triumph over me.*
>
> *And as for me, thou upholdest me in mine integrity, and settest me before thy face for ever.*
>
> *Blessed be the Lord God of Israel from everlasting, and to everlasting. Amen, and Amen.*

He flipped back a few pages,

> *Evil shall slay the wicked, and they that hate the righteous shall be desolate.*

So, he thought, there were two kinds of emptiness, one belonging to the wicked, one to the righteous. No matter what, one was destined to emptiness. It was simply a matter of choosing which kind. He flipped some

more, until another passage, this one in Proverbs, commanded his attention. It struck him as related to the previous verse about desolation.

> *The curse of the Lord is in the house of the wicked, but he blesses*
> *the habitation of the just.*

If he was not mistaken, this meant that desolation was not solely a matter
of the individual soul. It extended to the whole household. Those without
God were a void within, a state of desolation reflected in their house's
emptiness. Those with God were a receptacle for his presence, a state
equally reflected in their house's fullness.

Two

I n November, he found a viable job. To be sure, it was an odd job. But odd is what he needed, since it would provide him the flexible schedule necessary, in order to prioritize writing the book. It would be manual labor, which would allow him to be outside, and, best of all, it had no relation to the academic world, which meant that he would be unknown to everyone he met at work.

"What is it?" Alison asked.

"It's some wealthy family in River Oaks. They're looking for a driver."

"A driver?"

"Yeah."

"Like a chauffeur?"

"Partly. It looks like they also want me to run errands."

"Interesting."

"Yeah, I'm going to email them. It may just be a scam, but it's worth looking into."

By the time he received a response two weeks later, he was surprised. He'd written it off as a dead end. A woman had sent an email giving her name and a phone number. He was instructed to call it. When he did, the woman said she wanted to meet him at a Barnes and Nobles for an interview. There was nothing particularly strange about that. What was somewhat strange is that the location was relatively far removed from River Oaks. When he asked about that, the woman was evasive. He understood. It could just be that the family wanted privacy and to ensure its safety, by screening new employees in a location that wouldn't disclose the home. The woman set a time and date for the interview, and he agreed to be there.

He arrived a little early. He took a seat at the café which was empty. After waiting a while, he bought a coffee. He checked the time. The woman was already ten minutes late. He finished the coffee, and she was still not there. Waiting in a book store wasn't so bad at all. He flipped through some of the titles while keeping an eye on the café. She was a half hour late, and he was beginning to think she wasn't coming. He could leave, but something told him to stay, so he returned to the table. Finally, forty-five minutes late, a Mexican woman in business attire appeared.

"Sorry about the wait," the woman said. "I'm Angela." He gave his name.

"You're interested in working for the family?"

"Yes."

"Have you done a job like this before?"

"Driving? No."

"You have a clean driving record?"

"Oh, yes. Not even a traffic ticket!"

The woman smiled. "That's good. Yui will like that. She's very protective over the children." Angela, assuming that were truly her name, must have sensed that he was wondering what her true intentions might be. For all he knew, she was a scam artist.

"I'll tell you more about the family in a minute. I just have to ask you some preliminary questions, first."

"Okay."

"You have a license?"

"Yes."

"You're a citizen?"

"Yes."

"You have no criminal record?"

"Yes."

"You have a flexible schedule?"

"Yes."

"You have references?"

"Yes."

"You don't mind working with kids?"

"No, not at all. I'm a teacher," he said.

"Teacher?"

"Well, yes. I've taught university classes in the past."

"University?"

"Yeah."

"Oh, good, so you're smart. You'll figure out the job. A lot of what I can tell you is obvious. But I'll give you some pointers about the family.

I can't tell you too much, though, until you've signed the NDA." She was about to move on, when he saw that something had occurred to her.

"If you've taught at university, why are you looking at this job?"

"Very long story. I'm working on a book right now, so a job like this will be something I can work around my writing schedule."

"Oh, I see. Well, I'll mention this in a minute, but you should be warned. The family is very demanding. They expect their employees to put in a lot of hours. If you take the job, you'll have to learn to set boundaries. They'll ask you to do something, and if you do, it'll be your new duty. And they'll just keep piling new things on top of the others. If you don't know how to say no, you'll get buried. You have to know it's fine to say no."

"Okay." It sounded foreboding yet intriguing at the same time.

"Yui is very passionate about two things. Her kids, and her dogs."

"Dogs?"

"Yes, she has four of them. Three big ones and a very little one. German Sheppard's and a Shih Tzu. Are you okay with dogs?" He recalled his childhood dog, the scruffy Jack Russell Terrier.

"Yeah."

"Okay, good. She adores her dogs." He noticed there was no mention of a husband yet.

"Yui is divorced. The husband lives in the area. You'll be working with him occasionally, transporting the kids between places."

"Okay."

"Any questions?"

"Well, other than driving the kids to school or whatever, what else might I be asked to do?"

"As mentioned, you'll drive the two younger kids to school. The older one needs rides occasionally also. He doesn't have a license."

"Okay."

"Other than that, it's hard to say. It's really up to Yui. She always has projects and things going on around the house, so you'll have something to do. The exception is when they take a family vacation. They take big trips twice a year, one over summer, the other over Christmas. You'll be helping them prepare for those."

"Okay."

"Any other questions?"

"What's the next step? Will I start soon, if I'm hired?"

"Yes, you'll be starting very soon. This was just an initial screening, though. You'll have to talk to the lawyer next."

"Okay, sounds good. Thanks for taking the time to meet with me," he said.

"You're welcome. Thanks again for your patience waiting on me. Somebody from the law office will be in touch with you," she said.

Her showing up late, obviously, had been by design. If he had left early or been upset by it, he wouldn't fit the profile they were looking for. That meant they were looking for obsequious or patient types. He was certainly patient. He had nowhere to be, after all.

When he got home, Alison was on the couch.

"How'd it go?"

"Good, I think. They made me wait. I think they were interested in seeing whether I'd leave."

"How late was she?"

"Forty-five minutes."

"Oh, yeah, wow. Tell me everything."

He laughed, "You know I'm bad at summarizing things like that."

"Just tell me," she said.

"Basically, I drive the kids to school. It sounds like it's a crazy house with dogs and projects and constant bustle. So, I'll have a lot do. I can't say much more because I have to sign an NDA before they tell me anything, and I have to see their lawyer first too."

"Really? Interesting," she said.

His phone rang. It was from an unrecognized local number. He looked at Alison, "This is probably it," he said.

"Hello?"

A very civilized female voice was on the other end. "This is Catherine O'Dowd. I'm calling on behalf of the Dahley family. Angela has spoken to me about your interview, and she says that you seem to be a good fit for the position. Could you possibly make it to my office tomorrow afternoon at three-thirty?" A precise time, and on such short notice. Again, a test of compliance. He was comfortable with it.

"Sure, sounds good. I'd very much like to meet you. Is there any paperwork I should bring with me?"

"Yes, two valid forms of identification. We're going to want to process your tax paperwork as well."

"Okay, great."

"See you tomorrow." The phone clicked.

"That was her, the lawyer," he said.

"When do you see her?"

"Tomorrow."

"Tomorrow?"

"Yeah, they work fast. A family like that can move through as many employees as they want. There's always somebody else in line," he said.

"Makes sense. This won't interfere with your writing, will it?"

"No, not at all. I actually think getting outside will be good for me. Angela, the woman who interviewed me tonight, said that the hours are flexible. It should be fine."

"Should we celebrate? Let's go for fro-yo!"

"They haven't hired me yet! We'll go tomorrow when I'm back from the lawyer," he said.

Alison turned around from the couch to look at him as he walked to the kitchen. "Sounds good. By the way, are we going to do anything for Thanksgiving?"

"I didn't have any plans. I assumed we'll be here, right?"

"Yeah, okay, that's what I thought too. I'll tell my mom. My uncle and aunt from Phoenix are coming for a visit in two weeks. My parents are going to want to go out for dinner. Are you going to be able to make it?"

"Yeah, why not?"

"The job."

"Oh, don't worry. That won't be an issue. I can go to dinner."

He didn't tell her that he wished he didn't have to go, but he knew she knew that anyway. It was always a test in self-control to have to watch Linda and Stuart gaslight Alison, by pretending that it was perfectly normal for them to be living out here in Texas now after he had nearly been expelled from Oxford over nothing, and had his viva sabotaged. As frustrating as it was for him to have to take it, he knew in time, as things became even more obvious after he got the DPhil and then published the book, it would be Stuart in the uncomfortable position. One day, Stuart would be at a complete loss to explain how he had ever allowed all this to occur without ever once offering to discuss it, much less intercede to help. Stuart thought silence was his friend, but Stuart was simply digging himself a hole from which he'd never get out. He sighed. Trying times were ahead, he knew. But he would endure.

THREE

H E checked to confirm he had the correct address. The law office was located in the megamall complex. He never went to the mall, so he hadn't known the complex also included office space. He took the escalator to the top floor, and walked across an enclosed bridge, an uglier, more modern version of the Bridge of Sighs, that took him to the office wing of the complex. The law office had glass doors, where he could see a receptionist inside.

"Hi," he said, giving his name. "I'm here for an appointment with Ms O'Dowd."

"Yes. Please, have a seat in the conference room which is down the hall," she said gesturing.

"Okay, thanks."

He took a seat in a black leather chair and tapped his fingers softly on the mahogany conference table. He sighed. Evidently, he would be made to wait again like yesterday at the Barnes and Noble. It didn't bother him, or offend him. He didn't feel insulted. He wished he could just tell them that he would be fine with waiting on the job, so that he didn't have to wait here now, but he understood there was no way for them to know he was sincere. They had to be sure, so a dress rehearsal was necessary.

At four, the lawyer came in.

"Hi," she said smiling. She took a seat.

"Hi," he said.

"Okay, let me see your identification." He handed over some things which an assistant who'd also entered the room took to photocopy.

There was a pause as she looked through some papers. "I read through your cv. Very impressive. Highly unusual, too. You studied here?"

"I did."

"And then you ended up in Oxford?"

"Yep."

"And now you're back?"

"Yeah, I'm about to finish my DPhil. That's what they call the PhD there."

"I see. What brings you back here?"

He laughed, "Long story. My wife is from here originally, so we figured we may as well."

"Oh, that's nice. She has family here?"

"Yeah, her parents."

"And what do they do?"

"Her dad's a professor at the university. Her mom is retired. Former lawyer."

"Ah, well your wife must be very smart then, too. I will have to try reading some of your work some time. It looks interesting."

"Oh, thank you."

"So this will be a part-time job for you?"

"Correct. I'm working on a book right now."

"Congratulations."

"Thanks."

"Well, the job is challenging in some ways, but you'll surely manage. I'm sure Angela told you a little bit about the family," she said.

"Yes."

"Okay, well, the family is very private. So I'm going to have to have you sign this." She slid an NDA over the table. He signed it.

"And here's your tax forms." He filled them out. When he was done, he slid them over to the clerk.

"Great. There are three children. Tommie, Cheyenne, and Ella. Tommie, the boy, is the oldest. He's at college. St Thomas. You may be driving him to classes because he doesn't have his license. Cheyenne is a junior this year. Very smart. You'll be picking her up from school. Then there's Ella, the youngest. She's a freshman."

"Okay."

"Yui's parents live down the street from her house. Sometimes you might be asked to drive for them also. But not often. They have their own staff."

"Okay."

"Has anyone told you about the warehouse?"

"The warehouse?"

"Yes, Yui keeps a number of things in storage. From time to time, you might be asked to go out there and get something. Can you lift fifty pounds?"

"Yes."

"Okay, good," she said making a note on her pad.

"Do you have any medical issues?"

"No."

"Okay, perfect."

"You will learn more in working there, but I can tell you a bit about the family, since you're the sort of person I can tell will be interested to know. Some of the others who work there, as you might imagine, aren't exactly the curious type." She laughed.

"Sure, I'd like to know more."

"I mentioned Yui's parents. She also has an older brother. He lives down the street as well in his own estate, between the parents and Yui. Yui and her brother are now the owners of a local Honda plant. Her dad, who is old now and retired, spent some time in Japan after WWII. He met his wife there, and they eventually had Yui, the youngest sibling. That's where the name comes from. Anyway, Yui's dad has an aviation background. He got involved with the airlines, and after that, he got into cars. They have a plane that you'll probably be asked to load at some point. They take family trips."

"Okay, sounds good." He thought about the day at the Prison Museum and the lake. The same thoughts he'd had about Manzanar and Tarawa and the Indianapolis began surfacing. It was all absurd. Here, after all, was a Texas family running a Honda operation based on the business connections the patriarch had formed in Japan shortly after the war. All those men had died on those islands, and then it was as if nothing had happened. It was all business. What a waste, he thought, sighing.

"Is something wrong?"

"Oh, no. Sorry," he said.

"Okay, well, unless you have any questions, I think we're set."

"No, I don't think so."

"Okay, take this number. It's Michelle's number. That's Yui's main assistant. You'll want to work out a schedule with her. You've picked a rather hectic time of year to start. They just had Halloween, now they're organizing for Thanksgiving, and then it will be Christmas decorations. Yui loves Christmas. It's the big one each year," the lawyer said.

"Okay, thanks." They stood up and shook hands.

In the parking lot, he dialed the number. It rang twice and an exasperated voice answered.

"Yeah, hello?"

"Hi," he said, giving his name. "I was just hired to work for the family."

"Okay."

"The lawyer told me to call you to work out a schedule."

"Right, of course. Sorry. It's just very busy here today. I didn't mean to be rude," she said.

"That's fine. I'm sorry to interrupt." He could hear loud voices from what sounded like workmen. There were sounds of hammering and sawing. Someone came up to the woman on the phone.

"Not now, not now," she said. "I'm on the phone, can't you see? I already told you! Yui says Jorge and Javier need to use the stuff we just got from Home Depot. Burris left it downstairs. Tell them to go find it."

There was a pause.

"Sorry, sorry about that. Someone had a question here."

"That's fine," he said.

"Can you come tomorrow?"

"Yeah."

"Okay, I'll have Regina call you."

"Who's Regina?"

"Regina is the one who runs some of the things for Yui. She coordinates the kids' schedules. She'll talk to you."

"Okay."

"Bye," Michelle said.

"Bye," he said. He heard a cacophony on the other end before the line cut out.

That night, Alison and he walked under the oaks to the small shopping center for yogurt. The Chinese Consulate was in the lot over. He shook his head. Thinking about the absurdity of geopolitics and warfare was useless. The same fraud was perpetrated over and over. Governments sucker their young men into thinking they're fighting for a noble cause, and the only result is business contracts and profits for those who were invested behind the scenes. It had happened with WWII, it had happened after the Cold War, and now it was happening with China. His own family was a case in point. Stuart takes US taxpayer dollars coming from the US military and does research that he in turn shares with the Chinese. So, in effect, the American people were funding research and development for the Chinese military. This was not a secret. It was done in the open at the university, with the administration's full approval, as if there were nothing strange about it. He sighed.

"Is something wrong?"

"No, sweetie. I was just thinking."

They went inside and ordered, then took a seat at a table outside.

"It's nice out for November," he said.

"Yeah," she said.

They took some bites.

"So how did the meeting with the lawyer go?"

"It went fine. Signed all the paperwork. I called the house there today. Someone is supposed to contact me. Looks like I might be going in tomorrow."

"Your first day!"

"Yep," he said laughing.

"Tell me about the family." He told her everything he could remember. About the dad and Honda, Yui and her brother, and the three kids.

"What about the husband?"

"I don't know much about him. Angela, the one who interviewed me at the Barnes and Noble, said he lives in the area. I might meet him eventually."

"Weird. So they all have their own staff?"

"Yeah."

"What do you think they do all day?"

"I guess we're going to find out!" he laughed.

Alison got a look on her face. "How old are the girls?"

"They're high schoolers. Freshman and a junior," he said.

"Uh, huh. I see," she said.

"Oh, give me a break. They're kids."

Alison laughed, "You know about Chip!"

"Yes, well, I'm not your perverted high school teacher, who hit on you and the other girls." Alison's high school English teacher, Chip, had made a point of telling many of the girls at the school that his favorite book was *Lolita*. There had been rumors, too, that he'd ask some of the girls to take photographs for him and even make films.

She laughed. "I'm just joking," she said.

"I know." It was a potential issue he had already thought about. Trying to be holy didn't make him naïve. It just meant dealing with the lusts of the world differently than how those who did not want to be holy dealt with them. If he were driving the girls around, that would mean some-times being alone with them. He would take extra precaution to be as polite and respectful as possible. In all likelihood, they were already sub-ject to all sorts of sexualization at school and elsewhere. That's how the culture was. He would do his best to be a counterexample to all that, by being a man who valued whatever was left of their innocence, and treated them honorably, without any sort of ulterior, unscrupulous motives. The fact that they were coming from a divorced household must only compli-cate things for them, he thought. He had looked the family up. They were worth billions. Being that rich could present just as many problems, if not more, than being poor. It must be alienating to be that rich.

A young man in his twenties, with a crew cut, emerged from the Consulate and walked into the parking lot.

"That's strange," he said.

"What?"

"That guy."

"What? The one getting into the SUV?"

"Yeah."

"Why?"

"He just came from the Consulate."

"So?"

"Well, he's white."

"And?"

"He's not a diplomat or business man."

The young man had on blue jeans, a black shirt, and combat boots.

"Yeah, so?"

"So why would he have been in there?"

"I don't know," Alison said.

She took a bite of her yogurt. "I talked to my mom."

"Yeah?"

"Yeah, dinner's two weeks from now on Friday. It's at eight, will that work?"

"Yeah. Where?"

"True Food Kitchen, it's on Post Oak."

"Oh, nice. That'll be right near me."

"Yeah, my mom picked a place close to your work."

"You told them about the job?"

"Yeah. They say congratulations," she said.

"Well, as you know, it's everyone's dream to parlay an Oxford education into driving a car for some random rich family out in River Oaks," he laughed.

Alison looked at him seriously. "You know it doesn't matter to me. I don't care what your job is. I love you," she said.

He stared into the parking lot, "I'm sorry."

"For what?"

"For this. It's not fair that you have to deal with the fallout."

"It's fine. We'll figure it out," she said.

"Look at that," he said.

"What do you think is in it?"

The man from the Consulate had pulled a briefcase from the backseat.

"Money," he said to Alison as they watched the man.

The man went back into the Consulate. A few minutes later, as they were finishing their yogurt, he appeared again without the briefcase, got in the SUV, and drove away.

"Weird," Alison said.

"That's how it works," he said.

"How what works?"

"Everything," he said.

FOUR

ITH him working in the afternoons, that meant driving
Alison to work in the morning, so that he could have the
car to drive himself to work. They couldn't afford another
car. He knew that if he asked, his dad would buy them one, but his dad
and him both knew it wouldn't be worth the trouble. His mom would
feel like his dad was babying him. Of course, if he ever tried asking his
mom why he was stuck in the financial situation he was, that would only
raise the situation in Oxford, a subject she was unwilling to discuss. His
mom had made up her mind that he was to blame for what had happened there. There was the further fact that, if his dad helped with the car,
Alison might resent it. After all, it would understandably remind her of
how her own parents had reneged on their promise to give her the money
for not having attended Wheaton. Alison might interpret his decision to
have his dad pay for the car as a way of slighting her own parents, which
she wouldn't appreciate, since her parents would see it too, which in turn
would only inflame tensions between her and her parents. Inevitably,
whatever ill-will his buying the car would engender in her parents would
be directed at her. In order to spare her their ire, he would not get the
car then. The upshot was that the schedule was unnecessarily complicated and inconvenient, but keeping what was left of the family peace was
worth the added hassle.

As he pulled up to the family's house, he parked out front. The entire
length of the property's front yard was lined with other parked cars. Must
be the rest of the staff, he thought. He pressed the gate's intercom.

"Yes?" It was Michelle.

"Hi," he said.

"I'll buzz you in." He walked down the driveway under the oaks.
The yard was massive, with a perfectly manicured lawn, complete with a

putting green and sand traps. There were azaleas, petunias, and hydran-
geas dotting the driveway. The house itself was a nondescript modern
two story, with a gaudy entryway. He could see the back of the property extending down the driveway. He was bad with judging space, but
the grounds must have been at least two acres. He got to the front door
which was locked. As he walked to the side of the house, there were men
standing in the bed of a pick-up truck unloading bags of mulch on the
driveway.

They stopped and smiled.

"Hey, mang, you new?"

"Yeah. I'm a new driver," he said, giving his name.

"Javier," the man said, pointing to his chest. "This is Jorge," he said
pointing to the other workman. Jorge waved and smiled. The side door
opened and an older white man wearing a baseball cap came out. He had
a big German Shepard on a leash. He walked up to Javier and Jorge.

"I'm washing the dogs again," he said. "You guys using the hose?"

"No, no," Jorge said, shaking his head. "You can use."

"Great, thanks, guys." The man paused. "I have to get Ella at three.
If Yui forgets, remind her that's what I'm doing. I'll finish with the dogs
when I'm back." Javier and Jorge nodded their heads.

The man looked at him. "Hi, I'm David," he said. They shook hands.
"You're the new guy?"

"Yes."

"You're driving?"

"Yes."

"Okay, well, in addition to the dogs and other things, I also do the
cars. When I'm back from getting Ella, I'll show you around."

"Thanks," he said.

"You're welcome," the man said. He chuckled and made an exasperated look. "It's crazy here, but you'll get used to it."

The man looked at the dog. "Oh, this is Bear. The other one inside
is Chief. Tammy, the other German Shepard, is at the vet right now. The
small mutt is Crystal."

"Okay," he said.

"Yui loves her dogs," David said. "Well, I have to wash Bear now.
By the way, nobody is supposed to wash Bear except me. He's usually
friendly, but sometimes he gets aggressive. If you ever need to do something with Bear, come get me," the man said.

He looked at Bear.

"Are you afraid of dogs?"

"No, not at all."

"Okay, good. Come on Bear, let's go," David said. They disappeared behind the back house. On the other side of the workhouse was the rest of the yard. There was a large pool lined with marble sculptures that he saw as he walked to the side door, which was locked. He turned to the guys in the truck.

"Ah," Javier said, jumping down. "There's a code." Javier punched it in, and he watched Javier's fingers, memorizing the sequence. Inside was a large kitchen with granite counters. There was a living room with photographs. Many, many photographs. They were everywhere. On the walls, and on the tables. He had never seen so many picture frames. The family was in every conceivable combination, these two girls, this girl and the boy, the boy and that girl, the girls and the boy, Yui and the girls, Yui and that girl, Yui and this girl, and so on. It was years of photos. Karate practices, baseball games, tennis matches, golf tournaments, graduation ceremonies, pool parties, beach vacations, Halloween costumes, and on and on. He had been in homes like this before. Homes that were only houses, not really homes. He thought it was telling that such places always went to the furthest extremes to try to appear to be homey. There were some photos of an older man, who must be the grandfather. He looked at some of the black and white photos of the man with others standing in front of a Honda plant. Black and white photos of the man in a cockpit. Black and white photos of the man when he was young, with a woman that must be the grandmother. Stepping into the house was like stepping into a museum, or a time capsule.

People were streaming up and down the stairs, many of them with headsets and walkie-talkies. When he got upstairs, a young blonde woman approached him.

"Hi, I'm Michelle," she said. She had her hair in a pony tail and was dressed in black business pants and a black collared shirt. She had tattoos on her arms, and she was clearly somebody putting behind a hard past. Evidently, she had partied a lot, and now wasn't, but it had given her a hard look. Within seconds of meeting her, her sense of ironic detachment from her surroundings was obvious. She was clearly smart. As he had pulled up to the house, he had seen her getting out of a dilapidated, old white sedan. She was struggling financially. Usually, it would be typical for somebody in her situation to be treating this as temporary, while she saved up for school. But that didn't seem to be the case here. He could tell she was uneducated, but she was uneducated, he judged, because she had seen that it wasn't worth going into debt. He wanted to tell her that she was right, that higher education was a fraud, but he didn't say anything.

She shook her head. "This place is nuts. Do you have the door code?"

"I think so," he said.

"Okay, good." Someone was chattering on the radio.

"No, no! They're unloading the mulch right now. Yui said they're going to need to get more at the store today. The planters have to be done by Tuesday for the dinner. They can water the lawn later." She collected herself, "Sorry. Somebody always has a question."

Something buzzed on her. "Hold on." She spoke into her walkie, "Regina? Can you let Burris in? The gate's not working. He has more mulch from the store to drop off for the guys."

She laughed. "Come on, I'll show you around."

They came down into the living room. "This is where Yui keeps the photo albums." She walked over to a table with a basket. "And here is where we keep the car keys." He looked in the basket, which was filled with handfuls of keys.

"I know, right? The keys are always going missing. Everyone knows the keys are supposed to go into the basket, so that others can find them, but it never happens. You'll notice that. Most of your job will be finding things that have somehow gone missing."

"How many cars do they have?"

"Twelve, last I counted. Eight SUVs, two trucks, a Lexus, and the coupe. There's a van, too. Most of your job will be playing musical chairs with the cars. They're constantly having to be moved and rearranged around the property to make room for whoever needs which one."

"Do I wash them? Or just drive?"

"David and Javier usually do the washing. You might help some-times eventually."

"Okay. Am I given a list of things to do?"

"Sometimes there are lists. Other times not. Depends. Don't ask me on what. I still haven't figure it out myself."

"So, I just wait around the house?"

"Yeah. Except, don't say that. Yui wants everyone to be busy. So even if you're not doing something, pretend that you are."

"Okay, who are the others?"

"You met Javier and Jorge outside. They do the yardwork and construction projects. There's also Juan. Juan's the foreman. He's been working for the family for twenty years. Enrique does the photos and electronics. There's Regina, who is Yui's mom's old friend. She lives here in the house and helps with the kids. There's Paul, Tommie's tutor. There's Casey. She's another personal assistant. Then we hired some new people. There's you. And also Theresa. Did I mention Burris? He's a driver."

"What does she do? Theresa?"

"She's going to be an assistant."

"Okay."

"Did you meet Burris?"

"No."

"Like I said, he's another driver. He's been working for Yui for twenty-five years. I think he's retiring soon."

"Okay."

"Then there's a bunch of other people that are around the house to help. You'll meet them all, eventually."

"Okay. Where's Yui?"

Michelle pointed down the hall. "She's in her room. She's busy right now. They're preparing for an event here on Tuesday. It's a party for Cheyenne."

There was shouting coming from a room farther down the hall.

"Will somebody call Ella? I need to talk to her!"

"Who's that?"

"Regina . . . "

Michelle's walkie-talkie went off.

"Michelle?"

"Yes."

"This is Regina."

"I know, Regina."

"Have you seen Ella? I can't find her."

"She's not here right now. She's at practice. Burris is going to pick her up."

He interjected, "Um, Michelle, maybe the plans changed. But I just heard David outside saying was going to pick up Ella. He was washing Bear."

Michelle was surprised. "Really? Oh, okay, good to know." Michelle lifted up the walkie-talkie. "Never mind, Regina, David's doing it."

"I don't care who is picking her up. I just need to talk to her. Yui said I have to talk to her about her grades," Regina said.

"Yes, Regina," Michelle said, smiling at him.

"Is there gas in my car?"

"I don't know, Regina. You'll have to ask David when he's back," Michelle said.

"I have an appointment at five. I have to go to the vet to get Tammy."

"I'll make sure you have gas, Regina," Michelle said.

Michelle looked at him, "Could you go check to see if the White Explorer has gas? The keys should be downstairs."

He went down the stairs, as a middle-aged man was coming up the stairs with a young man. The young man was shirtless and in shorts and sandals. That must be the son, Tommie. The two nodded at him, and walked down the hallway. Back in the living room, he fished through the basket, and found the keys for the Explorer. He went out the front door, and checked. The Explorer was on empty. When he got to the house, somebody called to him from behind.

"Hey!"

He turned around. A Mexican woman in her forties was striding up to him with an angry look on her face.

"What are you doing?"

He had no idea who she was. Presumably she didn't know him, either.

"Just checking the Explorer for gas. Regina has an appointment, and Michelle sent me down here."

"No using the front door. Yui said not to do that."

"Oh, I'm sorry. I'm new and nobody told me," he said.

"That's fine. Be more careful next time," she said.

Michelle came out the front door. "How's the car?"

"It's on empty," he said.

"Of course," she said. "Can you fill it up?"

"Sure."

Michelle looked at the woman. "I thought you weren't working to-day, Theresa?"

"No, no, I am. Yui texted me to come in. She says she's working on something very special and needs my help." Theresa walked through the front door into the house. When the door closed, he turned to Michelle.

"So, that's Theresa," Michelle said with a knowing expression on her face.

"Are we allowed to use the front door or not?"

"Yes and no," she said laughing. "Things here turn on a dime. It takes forever for an instruction to get to you. You'll just have to get used to things not making sense. The Explorer, for instance, is on empty. Regina's known about the vet appointment for a week. David's supposed to watch the gas. Now he's gone off to get Ella, and there's no gas in the Explorer, and of course Regina doesn't check until right before she has to go."

"Why doesn't Burris go to the vet?"

"Because Yui wants him to get more mulch from Home Depot."

"Oh," he said.

"Do you have a card?"

"A card?"

"For the gas."

"No."

"Okay, I'll talk to Yui about that. You're going to need to get a Costco card. Do you know the Costco nearby?" She pointed.

"Yeah."

"That's the gas station we use."

"Okay."

"You'll need a card anyway, because sometimes you'll be getting things from there."

"Okay. Do any of the other cars need gas?"

"David will check," she said. He didn't have to point out that obviously David hadn't checked Regina's car. "We'll get you a Costco card tomorrow. For right now, use mine," she said, handing him a card.

"Thanks." He got in the Explorer and left the estate. On his way over to the gas station, he had time to organize what he'd seen. Yui was an eccentric recluse. Judging by what he'd already seen, the fact that she had a warehouse meant she was probably a hoarder also. She had hired a full staff of workmen and assistants to turn the ordinary obligations of life into a business enterprise. Rather than running errands, she had drivers. Rather than picking up her kids from school, she had drivers. Rather than doing the yardwork, she had gardeners. Rather than putting on things for her kids, she had event planners. The point wasn't to simplify things, the point was to give Yui something to do all day. Since she was a billionaire who didn't have to work, she spent her time creating schedules and orchestrating a legion of employees through unnecessarily complicated itineraries, governed by a fleet of assistants who only introduced further miscommunications and errors. The family were deeply bored people who had turned living into a badly choreographed routine. He had seen Tommie. He didn't look malicious or arrogant. He looked childish, in a stunted way. He probably hardly left the house, and after years of being babied, he didn't have any of the basic skills a young man his age should have. He hadn't yet met Cheyenne or Ella, but from the sense he got, Cheyenne was the well-behaved one, whereas Ella was a bit of a trouble-maker.

He pumped the gas and stared across the parking lot. He never thought he'd find himself here doing this, but here he was. When he was done filling up the gas, he got in the car, and headed back to the house. Just down the street from the gate, his phone rang. It was an unrecognized number.

"Where are you?"

"Sorry, who is this?"

"Theresa. Where are you?"

"I'm outside the house."

"What are you doing?"

"I'm coming from Costco. Regina's Explorer needed gas."

"That's David's job. He does the gas."

"Yes, but David's picking up Ella. The car was low, so Michelle told me to fill it up."

"You don't have a Costco card yet."

"She gave me hers."

"Cheyenne called. She's stranded at school. You were supposed to pick her up."

"I was?"

"Yes, you're a driver. That's what you were hired to do."

"I'm sorry. It's my first day. I didn't even have a schedule. I was just told to come by, so I did. I didn't know I had anywhere to be. I don't even know where the school is."

"You should have asked."

"But why? Nobody told me I had to get Cheyenne today. Why can't David? Don't Ella and Cheyenne go to the same school?"

"They have different drivers. Cheyenne is coming straight home to do homework. Ella has an appointment."

"Can Burris get her?"

"He's at Home Depot."

"Okay, well, I'm about to drop off Regina's car. I can get Cheyenne after that."

"Hurry. Yui wants to talk to her when she's home." The phone clicked off.

He pulled up to the gate and pushed the buzzer.

"Yes?"

"It's me. I'm back from Costco."

"Who is this?"

He gave his name.

"Come up to my room, when you're inside."

"Your room?"

"Yes, I'm across the hall from Yui." He thought about it. This must be Regina, then.

"Okay." He parked the car next to the Lexus and SUVs. It might be faster to go through the front door, but after the scolding from Theresa about that, he'd use the side door. On the driveway, Javier and Jorge were carrying the mulch bags into the yard. Another man, who looked to be in charge, was helping. That must be Juan.

He stopped and faced the three men, pointing kindly at the other man. "Juan?"

"*Si*," Juan said smiling.

He gave his name, and they shook hands.

Javier looked at him, "Regina said she wants to talk to you," he said.

"Yeah, thanks, she just told me." He punched in the code to the door, and walked through the kitchen. Bear was on his bed, and growled at him, but when he reached the stairs, the dog settled down and closed his eyes. Tommie and the other man were coming down the stairs.

"The test is Friday. I think I'm ready," he was telling the man.

"Okay. I'll be back tomorrow night so we can review."

"Sounds good. I have to get dressed. I'm meeting some friends at the steak house."

The man walked down the stairs and stuck out his hand. "I'm Paul," he said.

"Good to meet you," he said, shaking his hand. "I'm a new driver."

Tommie looked down at him from the landing. "Are you driving me to the restaurant?"

"Uh, I don't think so. Nobody mentioned it. Theresa said I have to get your sister."

"Ella?"

"No, Cheyenne."

"I thought Cheyenne has practice?"

"Practice?"

"Yeah, golf practice." He knew from experience that golf was a Spring sport.

"Golf? It's November."

"She's on the team at school. But she also takes lessons at the country club."

"Ah, I see."

He asked Tommie, "Why does it matter if she has practice?"

"Because David drives Cheyenne to practice," Tommie said.

"But I thought David picks up Ella, not Cheyenne?"

"He does. He picks up Ella from school and then drives Cheyenne to practice."

"Why doesn't he also just pick up Cheyenne from school?"

Tommie smiled. "That's just how my mom wants it, I guess."

"Okay, well, I'm supposed to get Cheyenne from school now. I don't know whether she has practice afterwards. Somebody will have to ask David."

"Regina will know," Tommie said. Tommie started yelling down the hall, "Regina! Does Cheyenne have practice today?"

Michelle came out of Yui's room. Regina came over Michelle's walkie-talkie.

"Michelle? Where's the new driver? I need to talk to him," Regina said.

"He's right here, Regina. He's talking to Tommie. They're trying to figure out Cheyenne's schedule. Does Cheyenne have practice today?"

"Yes," Regina said.

"So, David's got her when he's back from getting Ella at school?"

"No, no, Burris is driving."

"Burris?"

"Yeah, there's a birthday party Cheyenne's going to after practice. David will be off by then, so Burris is driving her to practice rather than David."

He looked at Michelle. "If I'm picking up Cheyenne already from school, why don't I just take her to practice and then the birthday party too?"

"Good idea. I'll tell Burris not to worry about the party. That will give him more time at Home Depot."

"Tommie needs a ride to the restaurant," he said looking at Michelle.

Michelle turned to Tommie, "Weren't you supposed to get your license?"

He shook his head, "Mom said no."

Michelle sighed. "Okay, well, when David gets back from school with Ella, he can drive you."

"Um, Michelle."

She turned from Tommie to him. "Ella has practice somewhere too after school," he said.

Michelle got on the walkie. "Regina, Ella has started basketball?"

Regina spoke, "No, piano, I thought. I don't know. Ask, David."

"David's not here," Michelle said.

"Call him," Regina said.

"Why don't you?"

"I'm busy." Michelle rolled her eyes then looked at him and Tommie.

"Okay, David can drive you to dinner after he's back from taking Ella to practice."

"But I'll be late!"

"Well, that's too bad. Tell your friends you'll be a little late." Tommie stormed off to his room.

A voice came screaming from Yui's room as he walked by.

"Put a shirt on, Tommie! It's four o'clock."

He looked at Michelle. "That's Yui," she said.

"If David's driving Tommie to dinner after dropping off Ella at practice, who's going to get Ella from practice later?"

"Can you?"

"No, I'll be driving Cheyenne."

"Oh, yeah, that's right. Okay, I'll call Burris." She looked at him. "Can you get Tommie from dinner?"

"I'm not sure. Can one of his friends drive him back?"

Michelle yelled down the hall, "Tommie, can you get a ride home from dinner?"

There was silence.

"Tommie?"

Still more silence.

"Tommie? Can you get a ride from dinner?"

Tommie leaned out his door, as he was buttoning his shirt. "Yeah, I'll have a friend drive me." He didn't bother to ask why, if Tommie could get a ride from a friend after dinner, he couldn't also get a ride now from a friend over to dinner. Nothing made sense.

Theresa came out of Yui's room and walked over.

"What are you doing? Cheyenne is waiting!"

He looked at Michelle. "I have to go," he said. "Tell Regina I'll talk to her later. The Explorer is full, and I left the keys in the basket."

That night, when he was at the apartment sitting on the couch, the phone rang. Regina said he had to come by tomorrow to see her, in order to get his Costco card made and to talk about picking up Cheyenne from school. She was planning to drive him to the school and show him, even though he'd already driven over there this afternoon. There was no point in explaining that. He would let Regina take him through whatever routine she found necessary. He hung up the phone.

"Who was that?" Alison asked.

"Regina."

"Who's Regina?"

"I'm not really sure. I'll meet her tomorrow."

"Did you meet anyone else today? Tell me about it. What's it like there?"

He laughed. "This will take a while," he said. The phone rang again.

"What is it now?"

"Theresa."

"Theresa?"

"Hold on." He answered.

"Yes?"

"You need to come in tomorrow."

"Yeah, I know. Regina just called."

"Regina called you?"

"Yeah."

"What did she say?"

"That I had to come in tomorrow to get the Costco card and come with her to school."

"But you already know how to get to the school."

"I know."

"So why is Regina still taking you there?"

"I don't know. I'm just doing what I'm told."

"Tomorrow, make sure the cars all have gas."

"I thought that's David's job."

"No, drivers do the gas."

"That's not what Michelle said."

"I'll talk to Yui about it. Make sure you get Cheyenne tomorrow. She was upset about being stranded today at school." The phone hung up.

He looked at Alison and nodded his head. "See?"

"A Costco card? Who's David? And Michelle? Did you meet the son, Tommie? Why's Cheyenne angry at you? Is that the young one? Or is the young one Ella?"

He sighed. "Let me take you through it. There's a lot," he said.

The phone rang again. "It's Regina."

"She just called!" Alison said.

He answered. "Hello?"

"Tomorrow make sure the cars have gas," she said.

"Yes, will do. Theresa just told me about that."

"Theresa?"

"Yeah."

"Michelle's the one who's supposed to coordinate with drivers over gas. I'll have to talk to Yui about that."

"Oh."

"See you tomorrow," Regina said.

"See you tomorrow," he said.

He hung up. He was about to turn to Alison, when the phone rang again.

"Unknown number," he said aloud. He answered.

"Hello?"

"This is Yui," the voice said.

"Oh, hi Ms Dahley. I'm sorry I didn't have a chance to meet you today."

"Yes, it was busy. Tomorrow I need you to go to the lawyer. She has a package I need you to deliver."

"Okay. Regina told me I should come by tomorrow, anyway. She's taking me to school to get Cheyenne."

"Forget about that. David or Burris can do it. I need you to handle the package."

"Okay. What time should I come by?"

"Two," Yui said.

"Okay."

"Great, thanks. See you tomorrow." The phone clicked.

He was about to tell Alison that it had been Yui on the line, but before he could, the phone was rining. "Now it's Theresa!"

"Theresa? Who's this Theresa? She just called."

"She's the one at the house, who thinks she should be queen bee," he said.

He answered. "Yes, Theresa?"

"Yui needs to talk to you. Call her."

"She just did."

"Are you sure?"

"Yes, she just hung up."

"Yui has a package you need to deliver."

"Yes, I know. I'm to come tomorrow at two before heading to the lawyer's office."

He heard Theresa speaking in the room.

"Has he called you, Ms Yui?"

He heard Yui tell Theresa that she had just called him.

Theresa got back on the line. "See you tomorrow. Remember, two o'clock."

He turned to Alison on the couch. "Okay, so where were we?" He was about to begin taking her through the names and people at work, when she interrupted.

"It's okay. I can tell you're tired. Tell me tomorrow." She was right. He was tired. He looked over at his desk. He'd originally been planning to read the Levinas when he had gotten home from work. He'd get to it tomorrow.

"It's okay, sweetie," she said taking his hand.

"What is?"

"The job. If you don't like it, you can quit any time. You don't have to be there. I have a job." The problem wasn't Alison. He knew she would support him no matter whatever decision he made. The problem was others, who would mischaracterize his reasons for quitting. If he quit, he would have to find another job somewhere anyway, to keep them quiet, as he worked on the book. He thought about it. He would have to work here for a year. This time next year, he would be ready to submit the manuscript to the publisher. That would be around the same time as the academic philosophy job market. He would put in applications to appease Alison, who still didn't understand he was blackballed. But the main thing was the book. It was going to be a very long year at Yui's, but he could do it.

FIVE

H E got there at five minutes till two, and punched in. All the workers had to use a time clock in the laundry room. He walked upstairs in order to see Yui, when another voice came from the room across the hall. Someone was calling his name.

"Come in, I need to see you." It was Regina.

He went to the doorway and leaned in.

"Hi," he said. An old woman in her early seventies was slouched over a desk. The room was full with things from an earlier life, photos of a late husband, photos of her grown children, mementos from trips, old stuffed animals from when the kids had been young, and so on. Her purse was on the bed, and there were papers strewn everywhere.

She sighed. "I swear, I can't take it much longer with these people. Sometimes I think I should just move out. But I don't know what they'd do without me," she said.

"I know you said you wanted to take me to the school today to show me how to get Cheyenne, but Yui called me last night, and said that there's a package at the lawyer's office that she needs me to deliver to someone."

"Oh," Regina said with her eyebrows raised. He could see she was impressed that he would be entrusted with such a sensitive task so soon. Regina saw that Angela and the lawyer must have decided he was smart and could be trusted.

"Hold on," she said. She picked up her walkie from the desk.

"Theresa? Theresa? This is Regina. Are you there?" Regina looked at him. "Did you see Theresa when you came in?"

Theresa's voice came over the walkie-talkie. But he could hear her voice from across the hall, too. She must be with Yui in the room.

"Yes, go ahead," Theresa said.

"I have the new driver with me. He says Yui wants him to pick some-thing up from the lawyer's. Is that correct?"

"Yes, I told him last night," Theresa said. He didn't bother telling Regina that was a lie.

"Okay, well, I'll get Cheyenne myself today. But this is the last time. I mean it. Tell Yui that," she said.

Nobody dared point out the obvious, which was that the most natu-ral solution would be for Yui to get Cheyenne herself. Nobody would dare say so, because if the gratuitousness of any one task were ever to be questioned, no matter how inane it was, then the entire web of foolish-ness would be shredded, and everyone would be out of a job. The famous lines from Fitzgerald about the rich came to mind.

> Let me tell you about the very rich. They are different from you and me. They possess and enjoy early, and it does something to them, makes them soft where we are hard, and cynical where we are trustful, in a way that, unless you were born rich, it is very difficult to understand. They think, deep in their hearts, that they are better than we are because we had to discover the compensations and refuges of life for ourselves. Even when they enter deep into our world or sink below us, they still think that they are better than we are. They are different.

From what he was seeing, the very rich were different. As for this rich family, they were very neurotic. All the typical foibles of family life were expanded to cartoon proportions. In a way, then, perhaps they re-ally weren't so unlike the rest of us, he thought. It was the same human problems, only magnified.

Regina could see his attention was elsewhere.

"Is something wrong?"

"Oh, no, I'm fine," he said.

She waved her hand towards the room across the hall. "Okay, well, go see Yui," she said.

He left the room and entered the other one. There was a king bed on the left wall, with luggage, and shoes, and plastic boxes strewn across the room. A number of assistants were sitting on the floor, evidently organiz-ing the contents. The room itself was otherwise sparse. It certainly wasn't ornate. Just some plain carpeting and a few forgettable paintings.

A slightly overweight tan woman with dark red hair was sitting in bed. When she saw him, she stood up gingerly, adjusting her back brace. He noticed prescriptions on the nightstand.

"Boy, I'm glad to see you. I need you to take the package to the address. Here's the address." Yui handed him a piece of paper. "Do you know how to get there?"

"Yeah."

"Good."

"I'm going to have to find someone to get Cheyenne from school," she said.

"Regina just said she'd do it today," he said.

"Okay, beautiful. That makes things much easier." He could see she was beginning to think aloud. "Now I can have Regina take Cheyenne to golf practice, too. That will free up David to pick up the light fixtures . . ." Yui turned to a young elfin woman he had not seen yet. She was very pale, with light blue eyes, and white blond hair. "Casey, could you call David for me?"

"Yes, Yui," the assistant said. She looked at him. "Hi, I'm Casey."

"Hi," he said, sticking out his hand. He gave her his name.

Just then, Tommie came into the room.

"Mom, can I have Alan and Pete over?"

"Sure, but no more than that now. I don't need a repeat of last time." He looked over at Casey who blushed—evidently something embarrassing had happened here recently at the house with Tommie and the friends.

"Okay, thanks, Mom," Tommie said.

"Are you ready for your test on Thursday?"

"You mean Friday?"

"Yeah, sorry, Thursday, I mean, Friday." He looked over at the pills on the nightstand.

"Yeah, I'm ready. Paul's coming over tonight."

There was no evidence, of course, only a hunch, but he had the sense that Paul was probably paid to do Tommie's school work. They might even had found a way to have Paul help Tommie cheat on the exams. It was absurd, when one thought about it. Tommie clearly wasn't a scholar, so grades didn't matter. He wasn't the type who'd be going off to graduate school. And he certainly didn't need a job. He was a billionaire. Caring enough about grades to cheat made absolutely no sense. Only, in a strange way, it did make sense. Here at the house, he was beginning to see, everything was bizarre, to such an extent, that the bizarre became normal. Maybe it did make sense, then, that a billionaire party boy would be paying a tutor to cheat on school work at his middling college, so that he'd get a degree he had no use for anyway.

Yui faced him. "Call me when you've made the delivery. I may have some things for you to get when you're out."

"Okay," he said.

Yui turned to Theresa and Casey. "Have either of you seen Ella? I have to talk to her about her grades," she said. Nobody mentioned that Ella was still at school, and would have basketball practice soon.

"What car do I use?" he asked.

"Use one of the SUVs," Casey said. She smiled. Like Michelle, she saw the absurdity.

"Okay." He left the room, fished out the keys from the basket, exited the side door, waved to Javier and Jorge who were still busy with the mulching, and walked to the front of the house. There was no way to tell which of the SUVs might belong to the key, so he pressed the button. The lights for one of them parked next to the sand traps flashed. He walked over, got inside, left the estate, and headed toward the lawyer's office at the mall. The traffic was still light before the afternoon commute, so he was there quickly. He picked up a manilla envelope and drove to the destination, an office on the edge of downtown. As he drove over, he wondered what might be inside. Probably some sort of legal paperwork. He dropped off the folder, and called Casey. Casey was honest, so she would tell Yui that the package had been delivered successfully. If he told Theresa, she might not mention it to Yui.

"Hello?"

"It's me. I dropped it off."

"Great, thanks."

"Does Yui have anything she wants me to get?"

"I'll call you back."

After an hour, he started wondering whether they'd forgotten about him. The phone rang.

"What are you doing?"

"What?"

"This is Theresa. What are you doing?"

"I'm waiting on errands from Yui. Casey said she'd ask."

"Well, don't just sit there. Come home."

"But Yui said she wants me to run the errands when I'm out."

"Hold on." The phone hung up. Ten minutes later, Casey called.

"Sorry, I gave Theresa the list. Apparently, it went missing." So Casey had gotten the list of errands from Yui, and Theresa had never told him, no doubt to make him look lazy. By now, Yui would have been wondering where he was.

"Could you mention to Yui that I was waiting on the instructions?"

"Yeah, don't worry about it," Casey said. They hung up.

He read the list they'd texted. Mulch and spackle from Home Depot. They were very specific about the brand and other details, including the quantity. Six bags of mulch, eight cans of spackle. He looked behind him at the interior. It was going to be interesting to see whether everything would fit. Yui also wanted a number of new plastic storage boxes, presumably for whatever project he'd seen the assistants working on earlier. She wanted twelve of them, which wouldn't be a problem, if it weren't for the fact that she wanted the other items from Home Depot, too. He might have to make two trips, which would only add time, and after having already wasted as much time as he had because of Theresa, he couldn't afford to delay.

When he bought what he needed from Home Depot, he stored everything in the trunk to create as much space as possible for the plastic boxes. By now the traffic was terrible, because the evening commute had begun. The storage unit was in a part of town only accessible by highway or one of two major surface roads, both of which would be congested. He sighed, got in the car, and took one of the surface roads. After a half hour of traffic, the phone rang.

"Where are you?" It was Theresa.

"I left Home Depot."

"What about the other things?"

"I'm on the way."

"Well, hurry. Yui's waiting."

He didn't mention that it was taking this long because of traffic, traffic he was stuck in only because Theresa had been the one to delay giving him the errand list after he'd dropped off the package from the lawyer. Theresa wasn't very smart at all. The fact that she'd gotten him trapped in traffic hadn't been deliberate on her part; it just happened to be a good stroke of luck for her. He laughed to himself as he rolled the car window down.

Everything was the same no matter where one went, he thought. Here was a job where the job was not the job. It wasn't about running the errands, or picking up the kids, or taking them to their events. It was about helping Yui distract herself from the problems in her life that she did not want to face. It was about a broken family sustaining itself through a deeply dysfunctional arrangement that only their exorbitant wealth could buy. In short, everything was a pretense. Only a handful of the people there did any of the work. For the rest of them, it was about cashing a paycheck, and they would get paid anyway no matter what they did, so there was no bother to work honestly. In a way, their lazy attitude made sense. They really weren't being paid by the family to work. Yui was paying for friends, for assistants to keep her company, and for drivers and workmen to relieve her of having to do what a wife and mother ordinarily would do. Inevitably, since nothing there was really about its stated purpose, things deteriorated into politics and scheming and backbiting. He laughed.

Yui's house was no different than Oxford, where everyone gossiped and jockeyed for position. Since nobody in Oxford really cared about scholarship but only pretended, the real action was in the personal intrigues. The life of the don was simply an acceptable social license to waste time and entertain oneself however one saw fit. It was the same here, only it was comical in a way the world could acknowledge. That, of course, was why the NDA was essential. Yui and the family knew how they lived was bizarre, so using the excuse of security, they hid what they did from others who they knew would laugh. People could say that Yui and her lifestyle was a fraud, that it was a thinly-veiled excuse to avoid problems she didn't want to deal with, but it had been the same way at Oxford. Deeply dysfunctional, unhappy people degrading themselves over the pettiest things imaginable, all in a pathetically transparent attempt not to face the reality of their own brokenness. The only difference was that the people in Oxford were socially respected due to the institution, so everyone pretended that their life wasn't a fraud. In some ways, that made what went on in the Strawson Room or the SCR even more pathetic than what he was seeing here at the family's house. At least the family knew to hide who they were. The people at Oxford gloried in their shame.

His phone rang. It was Yui.

"Where are you?" So, Theresa had been complaining to Yui about him, saying he was slow.

"I'm in traffic."

"Do you have the boxes?"

"Not yet."

"Not yet?"

There was a silence.

"I've added some things to the list for Home Depot."

"But I just left Home Depot."

"Go back."

"Okay, but that will take more time," he said.

Yui sighed exasperatedly. "Well, I thought I was in charge, but apparently not. You know what, forget about it. Just come home. I'll have Burris do it. Oh, on your way, pick up some frozen yogurt, please." She hung up.

He sighed. Two days on the job, and he was already pigeonholed as the lazy, incompetent one. There was now another problem. He had no idea where to get the frozen yogurt. Somebody might assume it didn't matter, so long as it was frozen yogurt, but not in this case. Knowing Yui, she probably had a very specific store in mind, and she probably had a very specific order too. Of course, Yui had forgotten that because this was his second day, he'd never done a yogurt run yet, so there was no way for him to know what to do. Because she was already forming the negative opinion she was of him, he couldn't call her back. She would find it irritating, and see him as a further nuisance. But if he improvised and got the frozen yogurt from just anywhere, his mistake was sure to be noted. There was a dilemma. An inane one, but still a dilemma.

He called Casey. "Yui wants frozen yogurt. Where does she like to get it?"

Before he could tell her not to, Casey spoke to Yui. "Yui, what flavor do you want?" So Yui would think he was incompetent, but at least she would get what she wanted.

"She wants nonfat pineapple. No nuts," Casey said.

"Okay. From where?"

"Pinkberry."

"Okay, Pinkberry it is," he said.

Thankfully, there was no line at the store. When he walked in, he realized the next problem. He didn't know what size to order. Again, it wasn't the sort of thing to leave to chance.

He called Casey. No answer.

"Hi, sir, can we help you?"

"Um, sorry, just a second," he said.

He waited five minutes and called again. Still no answer. By now the staff was assuming he was here to meet somebody. They would think he was being stood up on a date. They had no way of knowing he was an Oxford graduate student running errands for a local eccentric billionaire.

Theresa called. "Yui is waiting on the yogurt!"

"I'm very sorry. I was calling Casey to see what size Yui wanted."

"She always orders a large."

"Okay, but I had no way of knowing that."

"They're all in the freezer."

"Okay, but I didn't know that."

"You should have called."

"I did. I said I'm waiting to hear from Casey."

"Casey's not here. She clocked out."

"Okay, well Casey didn't tell me that. She told me to get the frozen yogurt, so I did. When I got there, I realized I didn't know what size Yui would want. I didn't want to get the wrong order."

"Just hurry. You might have to run some more errands when you're back. Yui needs you to help Burris move something to the warehouse." He recollected what Angela had said at Barnes and Noble. He was seeing what she had meant. There was a never-ending list of things to do, since Yui sat around all day imagining new ways for those around her to stay busy, since it kept her busy. After the errand to the warehouse, there would be something else. That was fine, since it was his job, and he was being paid for his time, the problem was all the criticism that accompanied it from Theresa.

"Okay, I'll hurry," he said. Theresa hung up.

He walked to the counter.

"Hello, welcome to Pinkberry."

"Hi, thanks. A large nonfat pineapple, please. No nuts."

"It doesn't come with nuts," the girl behind the counter said. He sighed. There was no point trying to explain that he was ordering for somebody else who had told him to order it without nuts. He wondered how many drivers over the years had been forced by Yui to say no nuts, only to be told it didn't come that way. He took the yogurt, paid, and got back in the car. He sped to the house, where he buzzed the gate. Regina answered over the intercom.

"We've been waiting for you," she said.

"Yes, I know. I have the yogurt."

"No, it's Javier and Jorge. They need the spackling and mulch."

"I have it."

"Park the car in the driveway. They'll unload it there."

"Okay."

"I still need to talk to you about Cheyenne."

"Yeah, okay. I have to run to the warehouse with Burris, though."

"Burris is going to the warehouse? Yui never told me that," Regina said.

Someone behind him in the street was honking. He looked into his rearview mirror. That must be Burris.

"Regina, you have to open the gate. Burris is trying to come in," he said.

The gate opened, and they drove in the cars. He popped the trunk, and looked at Javier and Jorge. "The mulch and spackle are in the back. Do you guys want help unloading?"

"No, that's fine," Javier said. "Thanks."

He grabbed the yogurt and ran inside the house and charged up the stairs.

"Yui, I have the yogurt!"

Yui glanced at him disinterestedly, "Thanks, could you put it in the freezer with the others?"

"Oh, sure." He didn't mention the fact it didn't make sense that everyone had been telling him to hurry, only to find out she didn't even want it now. He walked down the stairs.

Bear was in the kitchen. He opened the freezer door, and his jaw about dropped. The entire freezer was crammed with frozen yogurt. Yui must have some compulsion with this too, he thought. He stuck it with the others, closed the fridge door, and stared at Bear, who was growling. He eyed the dog as he slowly backed away to the side door. When he turned the corner and went for the knob, he could hear Bear leap off his bed. He stepped out and shut the door just before Bear could chomp him.

Javier and Jorge had finished unloading the SUV in the driveway.

"Come on," Burris said. "I'll show you the warehouse." Burris was an overweight black man in his fifties. He was in a shirt with jeans, and had on big brown boots and a tan cowboy hat. He had a big smile, but something about it was forced. If Burris would be retiring soon, which is what he'd heard, there should be no competition between them as drivers. Frankly, he felt there shouldn't be any competition regardless. He had no desire to be Yui's top driver, and he wasn't aiming to show up Burris, by trying to do the job any better. He was happy to do what he was told, and leave it at that. Burris would see that, he hoped, and they could work together constructively.

They got in Burris's truck and drove over to an industrial district of the city that straddled a poor neighborhood.

"You want to make sure you lock the door and take the keys when you go inside the warehouse," Burris said. They walked to the metal door, where Burris made a call.

"We're here," he said to the man on the phone.

"Okay, one second."

"Who's that?" he asked.

"Tram. He handles security. He's the one who disables the alarm system."

"I see." There was a beeping sound, and then Burris lifted up the metal door. What he saw was shocking. In ten rows were giant gray plastic containers stacked from floor to ceiling. The shelves were old but sturdy. The warehouse stretched far to the back. At a glance, there must have been thousands of boxes. In addition to the boxes were Christmas decorations: reindeer, sleighs, elves, and so on. There were old French antiques and furniture. And there were rugs. Many, many rugs, all rolled up and stacked on each other. And there were also wallpapers. Many, many wallpapers, of all different styles. In containers in front of the rows were also rolled fabrics, hundreds of them.

"Never seen anything like it, eh?" Burris chuckled.

"Unbelievable."

"You want to know what's in the boxes, right?"

"Yeah."

"Everything. You wouldn't believe it. Clothes from when the kids were young, holiday decorations, just all kinds of things."

"Is it organized?"

He laughed. "Nope."

"There's no numbers on the boxes?"

"No."

"It all just sits out here?"

"No, we come out and find things for Yui."

"So how does anyone find anything?"

"You learn in time where things probably are," Burris said.

"What?"

"Yep," Burris said laughing.

"So, it's like a treasure hunt," he said.

"That's one way to look at it," he said, chuckling again.

It was insane. Yui would sit at home and have a memory of Tommie's fifth birthday, say. Somebody would be promptly instructed to go find the blue shirt from the memory. Next thing everyone knew, the house would be on a mission for three or four days rifling through hundreds of boxes looking for Tommie's old blue shirt from his fifth birthday party. Or maybe Yui was considering reupholstering a chair, so one would go through hundreds of the rolls, looking for the one fabric she was looking for. Or maybe somebody Yui knew might want one of the rugs, so it was the workmen's jobs to dig it out from underneath dozens of others, and take it back to the house. Often, there would be multiple search missions going on at once. Sometimes they would eventually lose steam and disappear without resolution. Other times the item would be discovered, but by that time Yui no longer cared. Stepping into the warehouse was like stepping into Yui's exteriorized living memory.

"Can I look in the boxes?"

"Go ahead. I'm supposed to get a rug," he said. Burris started searching through the rugs, as he began opening the boxes. Christmas lights, more Christmas lights, Halloween masks, old pool equipment, shirts, sandals, and straw hats.

"She always talks about getting rid of things. Never does. We actually just moved everything into this one. The old warehouse got too small. Every few years she wants a big reorganization. I get the feeling she's going to be having us do that soon," Burris said. "Ah, I found the rug," Burris said. They walked over, lifted it together, and gingerly navigated through all the clutter without tripping, tossing it in the bed of the truck.

"Let's go," Burris said. He got on his phone, "Yeah, Tram, we're leaving. Arm it."

When they got to the house, it was dark. Javier and Jorge were now working inside the guesthouse, applying the spackle from Home Depot. Evidently, they were being asked to repaint the interior. Casey had left, and Michelle was now here. He realized that he could stay here all night, and Yui would just keep finding new things for him to do. He decided it was time to go home.

He walked up to Yui's room.

"Is it okay if I go?"

"Yes, sure. Did Burris show you the warehouse?"

"Yes."

"Good, I'm going to be starting a big reorganization of the warehouse. I'll tell you more later."

He thought he would only be driving, but if she wanted him for manual labor also, that was fine. The absurdity here at the house was good for him, he decided. It was a spiritual test, something that allowed him to increase his patience and grow in grace. He had seen enough of the world to know it didn't matter where he was. It was the same. Watching Theresa play a game over an errand list was no different than watching Quiller play a game over the secondary literature in a confirmation meeting. When one stripped it down, a reprobate was a reprobate. If he embraced things here, he could grow in ways that would translate nicely to the academic arena when the time came to push the book through the publisher.

"Okay, sounds good. By the way, Regina got Cheyenne today. Should I pick her up from now on?"

"Yes, be here tomorrow. Two forty-five."

"Right."

He punched out, got in his car, and drove home. He knew he would be too tired to read the Levinas when he was home.

Six

THE next day, as he pulled the SUV up to the front of the school, he realized that this was right about when they'd all be walking over for dinner at Quod in Oxford. He laughed at the absurdity. From Oxford philosopher to child chauffeur. The moms were all lined up in their oversized SUVs. Many of them had gotten out to gab with each other while they waited for school to get out. Obviously, he wouldn't be joining them.

The verses from Peter entered his consciousness, "God opposes the proud but gives grace to the humble. And God will exalt you in due time, if you humble yourselves under his mighty hand by casting all your cares on him because he cares for you." He reminded himself it wasn't Cheyenne's fault that he found himself here. It wouldn't be fair to her to take it out on her. He would be positive and nice. He thought of the adults in his life who had said things that had stuck with him, even if it was only years later until he realized its significance for him. Maybe he would be able to do that. If in the next year or so that he was working here he could impart even just one good thing that Cheyenne might remember, that would be worth it. That will have been a success, he thought.

She opened the door on the rear passenger side.

"Hello," she said. "You're Mom's new driver?"

"Yes."

"I'm Cheyenne," she said. He gave her his name.

She had blue eyes and long, light brown hair. She wasn't wearing a lot of makeup, which accentuated her very prominent bone structure. He thought he had heard somebody at the house mentioning how the family had Indian blood. That would explain her name, after all.

"Should I take you straight home?"

50

"Today, yeah. On Tuesday and Thursday, I have golf practice at the club."

"Okay."

He drove out of the lot and got on the road. Occasionally, when he would check the rearview mirror for traffic, he would see her looking out the window, with her head on her chin. She seemed deep in thought about something. He thought about asking, but he didn't want to be intrusive. He wasn't sure whether he was supposed to talk at all or not.

"I have a question," he said.

She looked at him, "Yeah?"

"Your other drivers. Do they talk to you guys or not?"

"Usually."

"Oh, okay. Well, if you don't want that, that's fine. You decide."

"I don't mind if you talk to me."

"Okay."

They drove in silence for a while.

"Are you from Houston?" she asked.

"Oh, me, no. I'm from California."

"California? We have a place in San Diego."

"Oh, San Diego is great." He thought about his first girlfriend who had been from San Diego. That felt like a lifetime ago.

"Why are you here, then?"

He laughed, "Good question. I'm not sure. We were at Oxford. I'm finishing my PhD."

"Shouldn't you be there?"

"Another good question. Yes. But we ended up here instead. So here we are."

"Your wife?"

"Yeah, my wife, Alison. She's from Houston."

They talked about Houston until he pulled into the house. "Thanks for the ride."

"You're welcome," he said.

He felt sorry for her. It must be hard to have her parents divorced, and to have random strangers driving her around everywhere. He felt a tinge of guilt. This entirely bizarre lifestyle of Yui's only survived with employees. Maybe he should quit. Then again, if he did, she would only find someone else. But, still then again, that was the very excuse people always used to rationalize evil. He hated it when others did that. They exempted themselves from any personal responsibility by blaming the structure. The trouble was that society was so wicked and corrupt, that virtually any job of any sort involved one in some kind of structural evil, to some extent, anyway. If he worked at the phone store, he would have to sell phones made by Apple built by slave labor in China. If he worked at a grocery, he would have to sell cigarettes, and alcohol, and meat that had come from factory farming. If he worked anywhere, evil would be there. The human world was evil. Some words of Paul came to mind, and seemed instructive. "*I wrote unto you in an epistle not to company with fornicators. Yet not altogether the fornicators of this world, or with the covetous, or extortioners, or with idolaters, for then must ye needs go out of the world.*" This must be what Paul meant. One couldn't escape evil. The task was to find a way not to participate in it oneself. In any case, if he had not sold his soul for a bright academic future as an Oxford professor, he was not about to do so for this job. He would have to be honest with himself as things developed. If he ever felt like he should quit for moral reasons, he would.

He parked the SUV in the front, and he was about to open the front door, when he remembered Theresa. Going through the side, of course, would mean passing Bear, but he'd rather risk the rabid dog than have to listen to another lecture from Theresa.

As he was about to walk in, David came out of the guest house.

"I'm leaving early today. Someone's going to have to drive Ella. Can you do it?"

"Sure," he said.

David looked relieved, "Okay, great. Thanks. I'll tell Michelle. Oh, wait, that's right, Michelle's gone too. Okay, I'll mention it to Yui." He thought it was telling that David didn't apparently trust Theresa, either.

A few minutes later, David came outside.

"Okay, so you'll have to get Ella from basketball practice at school. After that, she's going to a friend's house for a birthday party. Here's the address."

"Okay, cool. Thanks." He got in the car, and drove the same way he'd just come toward the school again. He parked out front in the same spot and waited. Thirty minutes later, Ella came into the car. She had black hair and fiery green eyes. Cheyenne was cherubic and kind. Ella was fierce.

"Hi," he said.

"Hey." She didn't say her name or ask for his. That was understandable. He saw how from her perspective this was weird. She probably wanted her mom or her dad to pick her up, not a stranger. He had seen what was happening to her now happen to others growing up. It was what led people to become the adults they were. Life's pain and disappointment led to the hardening of the heart. It was a way of coping with having been let down. Better not to care anymore, people decided. There were two ways he had seen people respond to being let down, two ways of trying to love. But because they weren't rooted in the love of God, invariably these ways did not work. He had in mind the ways of sadism and machoism. To take the latter first, some internalized the pain they had experienced of being let down by hurting themselves in the hope of punishing whoever was responsible for the hurt. This never worked, of course, because the very people responsible for the initial wound were no more concerned about the gesture intended to make them feel guilty or sad than they were about what they'd done. This led to further pain and disappointment, which in turn led to further attempts to hurt oneself. He had seen it many times before, people he knew spiraling downward into a void of drugs and alcohol and other destructive things. They learned to love their misery, because it was a way of spiting the world that had hurt them. Then there were the sadists. These were the people who internalized the pain of being let down by channeling it into aggression against others. If they had suffered, others would be made to suffer. If their suffering had not mattered to anyone, they would make sure others knew that neither did their own suffering. Hurting others was the way of dealing with whatever had hurt them. Most of the academics he knew such as Stuart, Carrell, Quiller, and Klaus were the sadists. Ella was a developing masochist.

"I'm taking you to this address? Is that right?" He handed her the slip of paper.

"Yeah."

"Okay," he said. They drove the fifteen minutes in silence. When they were nearing the house, Ella looked up from her phone. "I need you to pick up my friend, Katie," she said.

"Okay. Where's that?" Ella gave him the address, and they made a detour. Ten minutes later, Katie hopped in. He immediately knew the friend was troubled. She was dressed very provocatively, with too much make-up on. She had a smirk on her face, as she sat down in the back seat. The two of them began giggling and texting with each other. When they got close to the house, Katie turned to Ella, "No, don't worry, there won't be any parents here." He looked in the rearview mirror, to see. He noticed that Ella was looking at him to see whether he had heard what Katie had said. Nobody at the house had mentioned anything to him about it yet, but judging by Ella's panic, he assumed Yui had a rule against Ella being at anyone's house without a parent there.

When they got to the house, Ella opened the door to leave.

"Do you know when I should be back?"

"I'll call you when I'm ready," Ella said.

"Okay." He watched the two girls walk up to the door. Another girl opened it, and let them in. The door shut, and they were gone. So, Ella had told Yui it was a birthday party, when it wasn't. There were no parents there. Katie had let the truth slip out. He wondered whether David allowed Ella to break the rules when he drove her. The rules really weren't the issue. The issue was that he didn't want to have any hand in letting a young girl do things he knew were wrong, things he had seen his friends do at that age, things that had set them down a bad path from which, to this very day, many of them had still never recovered. If Ella was going to fall into evil, he didn't want to drive her to its door.

He sighed and dialed his phone.

The number rang twice.

"Yeah?"

"I just dropped Ella off."

"Okay, great. She said the party's over at ten. Can you stay to pick her up?"

"Yeah, I can do that. Listen, there's an issue."

"An issue?"

"Yeah, it's not a birthday party. There's no parents here. We picked up her friend, Katie, and Katie let it slip out."

"Oh, great," Michelle said. "I know Katie. A little monster. Thanks for telling me. I've been telling Yui that if Yui doesn't watch out, Ella's going to end up pregnant." She hung up. He felt uncomfortable idling in front of the house, so he pulled up to the end of the street, where he'd wait for word from somebody.

The phone rang. Of course, he thought. It was Theresa.

"Yeah?"

"You drop off Ella?"

"Yeah."

"So, what are you doing now? Just sitting there?"

"No."

"So, you're running errands then?"

"No."

"So, you are sitting there."

"No."

"You need to find something to do when you're waiting on Ella."

"I'm waiting to hear back from Michelle about it."

"Michelle?"

"Yeah." He was getting a call on the other line. It was Yui.

"I have to go, Theresa. Yui is calling."

"Yui is call—" He hung up on Theresa before she could finish her question.

"Hello?"

"Tell me what's going on." He told Yui what he knew.

"Thank you for telling me. I'm going to call Ella. Go back to the house and wait for her to come out."

"Okay." He flipped the car around and pulled up to the curb outside the house. He stared down the street. He didn't want to have to see the kids looking out the window when they found out Ella was in trouble. He sighed.

Five minutes later, he heard the car door open and close. He looked in the mirror.

"Ready?"

"Yeah." They drove the twenty minutes to the house in silence.

At the gate, Regina answered on the intercom. "Is Ella with you?"

"Yes."

"I heard what happened. I'm going to have to talk to her, too," Regina said.

He heard Ella sigh exasperatedly in the back seat. He parked the car. He almost thought about saying something, but he held his tongue. She gave him a death stare, got out of the car, and slammed the door shut. He knew Ella would say she never wanted to be driven by him again. That was fine. He'd done her a favor, even if she was too young and dumb to know it now.

Someone had left the front door open, so he walked in and closed it behind him. If Theresa wanted to yell at him about it, that was fine. He took a seat in the living room next to the dining room, two rooms nobody ever used. He sat on an old couch and stared at the walls. There was some shouting and door slamming. Then a half hour later, he heard footsteps on the stairs. Somebody came into the room and switched on the light.

Yui sat down on a chair across from him. She looked tired.

"Thank you for telling us about Ella," she said.

"You're welcome," he said.

He could see Yui was embarrassed. He didn't know what to do. His mere presence was a reminder of the dysfunction all around them. There were so many questions he could ask. To begin with, there was the question of where the dad was in all this. Then there was the question about why Yui didn't simply do the driving herself. She could have drivers for errands, to be sure. But there was no need to have others drive the kids. Then there was the question of Ella's friends. It was clear to him this wasn't the first time Ella had done something like this. She was falling under bad influences. This was simply the first time that she'd been caught, or that anyone had bothered to point it out. He felt like he should quit right there. He had nothing to say, since if Yui wanted to ask him what she should do, he'd say she should put her family first. But his entire job description was an obstacle to that. Maybe she should just fire everyone in the house, he thought.

"I feel like I'm going to hell," she said. It wasn't a figure of speech. He could tell she deeply meant it. She was confiding in him because she had decided that he was somebody worth speaking to about it. Everyone else around her for years had been lying. This was the first time anyone had done anything out of genuine concern for her or her family in a long time.

He waited for her to continue.

"I try to be a good mother. But I know I'm not." She laughed. "I mean, you should see the other mothers in this neighborhood. They're drunks, sleeping around. It's a disaster. I keep to myself. It's lonely." She sighed. "It was easier when James and I were together."

There was silence.

She looked at him, "You're married?"

"Yes."

"How long?"

"Couple years."

"Kids?"

"No, not yet."

"You're the quiet type, I can tell. No more partying for you?"

"Yes, that's right."

"Is your wife looking for friends?"

"I think so. She gets lonely."

"I know a nice young couple, if you're ever interested in meeting them. The husband, Kevin, has known our family for years. He's the youth pastor at the church. You'll probably meet him one day. I can put you in touch." He knew she was just trying to be nice, but something felt off. The idea of getting dragged into the church system with all the spaghetti dinners and lake retreats wasn't something he wanted.

"Well, anyway, you think about it," she said.

He could tell that the initial shock of catching Ella was wearing off. And now that the relief was wearing off too, her initial gratitude toward him was shifting slightly into resentment. She probably regretted saying what she had about feeling condemned. She would assume that she had shown weakness, and now one of her employees would never see her the same. He didn't want to tell her that the way she was afraid he would see her now was how he'd already seen her. It was how he saw everybody. Everyone was immersed in social existence, with their roles and masks, but for him, it never had seemed real. The fact that she admitted how she really felt wasn't a revelation to him. He had seen already that her life was deeply painful.

"Is it okay if I go home?"

"Yes, time for you to get back to your wife," she said.

"I'll be back tomorrow to get Cheyenne."

"Thanks."

"You're welcome."

When he got home, Alison noticed his distress. She asked to hear everything, so he told her.

"Wow, that's good you told the mom. I'm sure she's glad you did. Ella will be angry at you, but you did the right thing. She'll appreciate what you did when she's older."

"I hope so."

"Cheyenne sounds very nice," Alison said.

"Yeah, she's a sweet girl."

"Is she pretty?"

"Alison, give me a break. She's a child."

"I'm just asking!"

"You have nothing to be jealous about over a high school girl. But yes, she is a pretty young girl. But unlike your old high school teacher, Chip, I'm not a pervert, so fortunately for you, you have nothing to worry about."

Alison laughed. "I know, I know." She got quiet for a second.

"What?"

"Oh, it's just that with Ella angry at you, be careful with Cheyenne. They might fire you if you upset both the girls."

"Yes, I know. But what was I supposed to do? I had to say something."

"I know, I know. That's fine. I mean, just don't bring up any weird subjects that normal people aren't comfortable talking about. You know, no big things about the meaning of life and all that. They don't have to know that they have Sartre driving them around," she laughed.

"Okay."

SEVEN

T HE next week went off without any fireworks. He would pick Cheyenne up, and drive her to golf practice. At practice, he would wait in the car and read the Bible, or take a walk around the park. Some days, he would go straight home after driving Cheyenne from school. Other times, he would work late, running other errands. Go to Home Depot. Go to the Box Store. Go to Costco. Fill up the cars. Drive Tommie to dinner. Find something in the warehouse. Store something in the warehouse. Theresa was always looking for mistakes, Regina always had a long story to tell, Yui was issuing contradicting orders that led to complete confusion and chaos, and yet, in its own bizarre fashion, there was an order to things. He saw the appeal it had to the others. Entering the estate was like entering a private world where they could escape the outside.

It was Friday, which meant tonight was the dinner. Alison had needed the car when he would be at work, so she had dropped him off. He waited outside the gate on the grass. When the headlights were coming, he stood up. She pulled up and opened the door.

"Hello," she said smiling.

He got in. "I'm sorry, I stink. I've been rummaging through the warehouse all day."

"It's fine. Nobody's going to care." They drove down the same street he took every day to get Cheyenne. They drove by the dreaded Box Store. Just ahead was the even more dreaded Home Depot. He sighed.

"Is something wrong?"

"No, I'm fine. I love you," he said.

"I love you too. Okay, well, they'll be inside." They walked to the entrance holding hands. Inside, they walked over to the hostess. Alison was about to give them the reservation name, when they looked over, and saw her parents and aunt and uncle seated at a nearby table.

"Oh, that's them there," Alison said. They walked over. Linda stood up from her chair and hugged them. "It's so good to see you two," she said.

He took a seat next to Stuart's left, and Alison took a seat to Linda's right, who herself was on Stuart's right. Because Alison was now on the other end of the table, it would mean he'd have to talk to Stuart and the aunt and uncle across the table. Her uncle was fine. He was in his fifties, overweight with glasses and a mustache, with salt and pepper short hair. His wife, Lydia, was very quiet. He didn't mind quiet people. But there was something odd about her, a certain arrogance almost. He had tried talking to her at his wedding, and it had been impossible. When he sat down tonight, the uncle, Carlos, immediately shot out his hand and said hello. The aunt said nothing.

"Hi Carlos," he said.

"Hi, how are you?"

"I'm good."

It would be very important that he not complain about anything tonight at dinner. Even typical griping about everyday life would be something Linda would later suggest to the aunt and uncle was indicative of his being a malcontent. The story, of course, was that he'd had trouble working with those in Oxford, because he was difficult to work with. He wouldn't play into that tonight. He looked at the menu, while Carlos asked Alison questions.

"So you're back from Oxford?"

"Yep," Alison said.

"How does it feel to be back?"

"It's good. But sometimes I miss it there," she said.

"Thanks again for the picture," Carlos said. When Alison had first moved to Oxford, Carlos had told her that he wanted a photo of the Headington Shark, a statue out past Cowley. They'd taken a photo and sent it to him, and, evidently, he'd loved it.

"Oh, yeah. I forgot about the shark," Alison said laughing.

Carlos turned to him. "So how does it feel to be back?"

"Good, I guess."

"You're working, I hear?"

"Yeah."

"Sounds like an interesting job. Some rich family out in River Oaks?"

"Yeah, that's correct." He was glad for the NDA. It spared him having to say anything more. "My main focus right now, though, is the book."

Carlos was puzzled.

"Yeah, the book." He knew Stuart and Linda wouldn't have mentioned it to anyone. He would let Alison see it, since maybe it would get her thinking.

Carlos asked, "What book?"

He turned to Stuart. "Oh, sorry, Carlos, you didn't tell, Stuart? Since you mentioned my job in River Oaks, I figured you might have mentioned the book too." Linda looked away.

"I'm writing a book right now. Did you hear the story of how it came about? It's actually pretty funny. I went to an event in Oxford—"

Stuart interjected, "So, Carlos, how are things at Raytheon?"

"Oh, they're good, Stuart. I'll get to that in a second. I wanted to hear about the book." Carlos turned back to him.

He continued, "Oh, right. Well, anyway, it doesn't matter how the contract came about. It's an intro to my field. I'm hoping it will be useful to students."

"And you're writing it right now?"

"Yeah."

"When will it be out?"

"I intend to have the manuscript to the publisher this time next year. So it should be out early sometime the year after that."

"Very, very exciting." Carlos looked at Alison, "You must be proud."

"Yeah," she said smiling. "You should tell Lydia and Carlos about New York."

Carlos glanced at him. "New York?"

"Yeah, I'm having my dissertation defense in January in New York. Should be fun. Remember my best man Andy from the wedding? He lives there. Maybe I'll get to see him."

"That sounds great. Good luck. So, what's the plan after that?"

"We're not sure yet," Alison said. "I guess he'll be applying for academic jobs."

"I wonder if there's something at Stuart's," Carlos said. The table was silent waiting for Stuart to respond. But Stuart didn't.

He looked at Carlos, "Well, I know Alison and I will be happy to go anywhere. We'll see what happens."

He waited for Stuart or Linda to say something about what had happened in Oxford, but when it became apparent that they weren't going to do so, he changed the subject. They had wanted him to bring it up himself, so they could reframe the matter later when he was gone. By not bringing it up, he was making it more obvious to Alison that her parents were unwilling to talk about it. She would have to decide for herself why they were avoiding the topic.

He looked at Lydia and Carlos, "So how long are you two going to be here?"

The rest of dinner went by as dinners do. When they'd taken care of the check, they walked outside to the valet. He was about to head to the car, when Linda walked over to him and grabbed his elbow. She leaned in and whispered, "I just want you to know how grateful Stuart and I are for everything you're doing right now after what happened in Oxford."

He looked at her without saying a word. It was the exact same taunt as her earlier one about how he should write a book about it. For a second, he thought about turning to the group, and bringing up the topic since she had just mentioned it. But then he paused. That's exactly what Linda wanted. At this point, there was no telling what Stuart and Linda might do. He could see Linda playing dumb here at the valet, claiming she'd never said anything just now to him about Oxford. Maybe he was hearing things. That would be the implication. Eventually, he knew, as the situation back in Oxford lingered, Stuart and Linda would have to transition from mere active avoidance to open animus. When they decided this had become necessary, the first thing they'd do was attack his credibility. By then he would have the DPhil and the book would be well underway. That would mean attacking the work would no longer be viable, as it had been back in Oxford. They would attack him directly, then.

When he didn't say anything, Linda continued, "Anyway, I thought I'd just say that."

"Thanks," he said. He looked at Alison who was now watching Linda and him. He could tell she was curious. Alison walked over.

"What are you two talking about?"

"Oh, nothing, honey," Linda said.

"Shall we go?" he asked.

"Yeah." She turned to Stuart and her aunt and uncle. "See you guys later." They waved.

When they got in the car, he could feel Alison was uneasy. She thought he was keeping something from her. He could tell she assumed that her mom and him had been talking about her. Linda had deliberately pretended not to have been talking about anything to arouse Alison's suspicions. He sighed.

"Is something wrong?"

"No, I'm fine."

"You don't seem fine," she said.

"What do you mean?"

"Don't get angry with me, I'm just saying that something seems wrong." He sighed again.

"See! That's what I'm talking about. You're always sighing," she said.

"Gee, I wonder why?"

"What are you talking about?"

He laughed sarcastically, "Are you kidding me? You don't know?"

"Know what?"

"Your parents!"

"My parents? We just had a great dinner," she said.

"Oh, I swear, your dad could stand up in the middle of Thanksgiving dinner with his dick out, and everyone would pretend he was just passing the drumsticks."

"Don't be crass," she said.

"I'm sorry, but I'm being graphic to make a point. The guy's a joke."

"What do you mean?"

He looked at her, "Johnny Gosch?"

"Johnny Gosch?"

"Yeah, remember the dinner at Natural Foods when you tried to talk about the Gosch documentary, and your dad stared straight ahead and pretended not to hear you. He did the same thing tonight."

"What are you talking about?"

"What do you mean? Look how many questions Carlos asked tonight about Oxford and my work and our future plans. How many times has your dad ever done that? Zero."

She was quiet. "So?"

"So? That's weird. Why is he trying so hard to do everything he can to ignore what happened in Oxford? I mean, doesn't he want to know why his daughter had to move home and his son-in-law now drives cars around, even though he's about to get a DPhil from Oxford?"

"My dad doesn't care. He wants to stay out of it."

"Doesn't care?"

"Yeah, it's not his responsibility."

"Not his responsibility?"

"Yeah, he can't do anything about it."

"Can't do anything?"

"Yeah."

"Your father-in-law flew to London, paid for a QC, and stayed there for six months. He's not a powerful physicist with friends at Oxford like your dad."

"My dad doesn't know anyone at Oxford."

He laughed sardonically, "Are you kidding me? Of course, your dad does."

"He says that he doesn't."

"Your dad actually told you that he doesn't know anyone at Oxford?"

"Yeah."

"Wow, I can't believe he'd lied to you like that. It's so obvious."

"What do you want him to do?"

"I mean, he could have sent a letter or made a phone call to somebody. He could have met the lawyers. There's many things. He should have done more than nothing. And what about now? He doesn't care what Carrell's doing?"

"Carrell? What is he doing?"

"I'm blackballed! Your dad's just going to sit there and pretend it's not happening?"

"What's he supposed to do? It's your responsibility. He's not worried about you."

"Well, that mentality itself is psychopathic. Having no empathy or concern for others is a form of pathology. But even if somebody wanted to argue that it's normal and acceptable for your dad not to care about me and my career, what about you? Doesn't he care about his own daughter? I mean, there are consequences for you too."

She was quiet for a moment. "So, what? You think my dad is plotting against you with Quiller and Klaus?"

"Yes, and don't forget Carrell! But in any case, at this point whether your dad's actually plotting with them or simply allowing it all to happen is a difference without a difference. For him to pretend it's not happening is unacceptable. It's bizarre. And I'm tired of it."

They pulled into the apartment's parking lot. The second he stopped the car, Alison leapt out and slammed the door. He sat in the car and waited for her to get inside. He looked at the vegetable garden. Trevor came outside into the courtyard and waved. He waved back. He got out of the car, and took a walk. When he came in, Alison was asleep. He looked at the Levinas on his desk. He was about to walk over and do some late-night reading, when Myshkin walked into the living room and hopped on the couch. The cat meowed.

"Hi buddy," he said sitting down on the couch. Myshkin rubbed his head on his arm.

"I'm in trouble, buddy. Everyone is very angry with me," he laughed.

"I can hear you." It was Alison.

"So? You are angry," he said.

"I'm not angry," she said.

"Neither am I," he said.

"Do you have work tomorrow?"

"Yeah, tomorrow we start the Christmas decorations."

"It's not even Thanksgiving."

"I know."

"Weird."

"I know."

He sighed and got into bed. He stared at the ceiling for a long time. Today was a day in which the trees had said nothing. He was at peace with it, though. Things are going to be hard sometimes, he thought. If it were easy, it wouldn't be the narrow way.

EIGHT

I T was cold out, but it felt good. A cigarette right then would be great, he thought. He took a sip of tea, and gazed at the full moon which appeared even closer than usual.

"Wow, look at the moon. It's huge," Alison said as she pulled up a chair.

"Howdy neighbors," Trevor said from below in the courtyard.

Alison peered over the railing down into the courtyard, "Where's Kyle?"

"He's inside sleeping. He had a big day today. Three walks. Speaking of which, I'm going on a trip. Would you guys be able to watch him?"

"Yeah, sure," he said.

"Okay, great. You going to be here tomorrow?"

"In the evening, yeah."

"All right. I'll bring instructions by." Trevor went inside.

Alison spoke, "What's on tap tomorrow at work?"

Everyone at the house had spent the last three weeks busy with Christmas preparations. Hundreds of boxes had been pulled from the warehouse shelves, loaded into the van, and transported to the house. There was a make-shift triage structure erected in the driveway, where the assistants unpacked the boxes, organized the contents, and then placed the items on the grounds and inside the house. Yui's memory for specific details was uncanny. A certain limited edition life-size Reindeer from 1992, a certain manger scene she'd bought in Switzerland from 2002—the treasure hunting never ended. He'd spent hours each day lifting, pushing, and pulling boxes in the warehouse. He was sore and tired. Finally, they had turned the lights on yesterday, and the house looked like an amusement park ride. The most astounding thing about it all, however, was what he was about to tell Alison.

"They're leaving for a trip," he said.

"What? But what about Christmas? All the work on the house?"

"I know. They spent weeks setting everything up, and now they're leaving. It makes no sense." Yui had Enrique and a handful of other assistants busy packing the bags while the others were working on the decorations. He had gone upstairs to Yui's room last night, to find dozens of luggage bags on the floor. They may as well have been taking the whole house.

"Where are they going?"

"Somewhere in France," he said. "I have to drive the van to the airport tomorrow."

"How are they going to check all the luggage?"

"They're not. They have their own plane." He thought about Klein, the one who had died in the crash on his private plane.

"Oh," she said.

"Yeah. Apparently, they have their own hangar at the airport."

"What time will you be back?"

"I'm not sure. Why?"

"My parents want us over for Christmas Eve."

"Okay."

"You don't have to go."

"I'll be fine."

"Okay."

The next day, he arrived to the house early. He helped load the van with the luggage. When they were finished, he could barely close the van door.

Michelle walked over. "Take-off is in five hours. You'll want to leave now, so the guys have time to load the plane. Do you know how to get there?"

"I think so. That's the address, right?"

"Yep."

"Okay, I'll go." He was about to take the van, when his phone rang.

"Yui needs you to get food for the trip," Theresa said. Rather than play cat and mouse with Theresa over a series of phone calls, he decided to walk up to Yui and speak directly. The staff was in the room packing the bags and running through their checklists. Yui turned to him.

"We need food," his boss said.

"What kind of food? Like snacks for the plane ride?"

"No, for the trip when we're there."

"Okay. What do you need?"

Yui pointed to Casey, who had a list handy. Casey walked over embarrassedly and handed him the list.

He read aloud, "Five hundred tortillas? Two hundred blocks of cheese?"

"Yes, they're for the quesadillas," Yui said.

"The quesadillas?" he asked confusedly , but Yui had walked away and didn't hear his question. So, evidently Yui wanted enough quesadillas to feed an army for a family trip to Bordeaux, France. Even if each one of them ate a quesadilla for every single meal, they'd only consume a fraction of what she was ordering. And of all the things in the world for a trip to France, why quesadillas? And why bring them? Surely there was food waiting at the estate in France. It made no sense.

"Here's the restaurant. Call me if you have any problems," Casey said.

He left the house, got in the SUV, and left the estate. The restaurant was crowded for lunch. The hostess turned to him, "It will be a half hour wait."

"Oh, I'm not meaning to eat in. I want to place a take-out order, please."

"Okay. What do you want?"

He cleared his throat. "I need five hundred corn tortillas."

The hostess startled, "Five hundred? Just plain?"

"Yes. Nothing else."

"I'm not sure we can do that."

"I understand. Could I maybe speak to a manager?"

"Sure. One second."

Five minutes later, a man came out. "Can I help you?"

"Yes, I have an odd request. I need five hundred corn tortillas."

"I'm not sure we can do that. We need the kitchen space to do other orders. It may take a while. All you want is tortillas?"

"Yes, well, not really me. It's for my boss. Listen, I can't go into details, but I work for a very eccentric family in River Oaks. They're preparing for a trip to France later today, and the mom has out of the blue given me this bizarre order. There's nothing I can do about it. I'm sorry."

The man smiled, "Yui? I thought it was her. Everyone around here knows about her. She has her people coming into all the stores with orders like this. I'll have a couple chefs focus on it. It'll take about a half hour."

"Okay, thank you so much." He texted Casey with the update. As the tortillas began arriving, he carried them in containers to the van. When they were all loaded, he paid, then drove back to the house. Theresa told him to unload the containers in the guesthouse. Somebody else would take them to the airport.

"Should I get the cheese now?"

"Yes."

He drove to the supermarket and shook his head as he was standing in the cheese section. He took almost every block of cheese, and slowly wheeled his cart to the checkout aisle. When he got to the register, the cashier and bagger were confused. They wanted to laugh.

"It's for my eccentric boss in River Oaks. Don't ask," he said laughing. They laughed.

He unloaded all the cheese into the van, then drove to the estate. Theresa told him Yui wanted the cheese upstairs in the room, so he and David brought the blocks upstairs. When he thought he was done, and would be ready to start loading the van for the airport, a woman, probably Yui's sister, who was also going on the trip, picked up a block.

Her face crinkled as she examined it. "These are very expensive." She looked at him. "Let me see the receipt."

He handed her the receipt.

"Yeah, this is way too much. You can get the store brand for much less." She handed Yui the receipt.

"Oh, wow. What were you doing? That's a fortune for cheese! You shouldn't waste money like that," Yui said turning to him.

"That's all they had."

The sister looked at Yui, "You should return these and get the store brand."

Just as Yui was about to heed her sister's advice, Casey intervened. "Guys, I'm not sure we have time for that. You need to leave for the airport soon, and you're still not done packing. The guys have to load the van, and he needs to take the van to the airport. I think the cheese is fine," she said. The two sisters looked at each other, and even though they didn't want to, they decided to forget about returning the cheese.

He looked at Casey who nodded her head.

When Jorge, Javier, David, and he were done loading the van, he got in and left the estate. He merged on the highway, and stayed in the slow lane. He took an exit for the airport, merging onto a small access road that led out to the private wing of the airport, and pulled up to the hangar. There were two men on the tarmac.

"Where do I park it?"

"Right over there behind the plane." He drove over and a man guided him to the spot. He climbed out and opened the back.

"Glad to see they packed lightly again," one of the guys cracked. They all laughed.

"Do you guys need me to help?"

"No, we'll take it from here," the man said. "You can check out the hangar if you want."

Inside the hangar were a number of planes from Yui's dad's private collection. There was an F4 Phantom, the Vietnam era American fighter jet. But the real prize of the collection, at least so far as he was concerned, was the P-51 Mustang, the WWII American fighter plane. His grandfather had flown one in the Army Air Corps. He walked up to the plane. When he had been young, he had loved air shows, especially the Blue Angels. Now, seeing the planes made him sad. They were undeniably beautiful specimens, but it was hard to square their beauty with their ugly purpose. Really understanding that they were designed to kill people made it hard for him to enjoy them. He walked out to the tarmac. The family was arriving in two of the SUVs.

The men continued to load the plane as the family boarded. Tommie waved to him. He waved back. The crew was aboard, and the pilots were running through the preflight checklist. A few minutes later, it was time to draw up the stairs, shut the cabin, and prepare to taxi. As he was about to walk to the van to leave, Yui stuck her head out the airplane door. She was motioning frantically to him. It was an emergency. He ran over to the plane, and climbed up the stairs, to where she was shouting above the roar of the engines.

"Wait right here," she said pointing to the platform.

A few seconds later she came to the door. "Here, take this to the house. We don't need it." He almost burst into laughter. Yui was holding a teal t-shirt in her hand. It was in one of the plastic bags she used for things in storage. He looked at her incredulously. He studied her face, and realized that she truly thought it made sense to hand him a single shirt they didn't need, after having packed dozens of bags.

"Okay," he said taking it. He walked down the stairs onto the tarmac and over to the van where the men were laughing.

"Yui really is something," one of them said.

"Straight up crazy," another one said.

He wanted to laugh also, because it was so comical. But he also found it sad. Only someone in deep pain could behave like this. He got in the van, drove back to the family's house, which was now empty, parked the van, and got in the car to drive home. He had to pick up Alison. There was still Christmas Eve with the in-laws to deal with.

NINE

SUMMER came. Cheyenne had gotten her driver's license, and although Yui still wasn't letting her drive herself to school on her own, soon she would. At that point, his services would no longer be needed. He had wondered whether that might mean they would let him go, but instead, in preparation for the change, he'd been assigned to take on other duties. He was now regularly washing the fleet of cars. David didn't seem to mind, since it let him focus more on the dogs. And he didn't mind either, since it let him be outside. Best of all, he was alone, and he didn't have to be involved with all the infighting in the house. When he wasn't washing the cars, he was spending time reorganizing the warehouse for Yui, attempting to bring order to the chaos there. And of course, there were the errands. Things were pretty much fine, except for one thing that had been nagging at him. After washing the cars, very shortly afterwards, sometimes even the very next morning, occasionally one or more of the cars would be dirty again. Nobody had driven the cars between the washing and when he saw them next, so it was a mystery. They would have a bizarre spotting effect, and the windows would be badly streaked. At first, he wondered whether he had been to blame. But he had washed cars before, and there didn't seem to be anything awry in his procedure. Hose the car down, apply the liquid soap with a sponge, hose it off, vacuum inside, and then wipe the interior and windows down with cleaner. The first few times it had happened, it would be only one or two of the cars, but now the number of afflicted cars was growing. He had tried to ignore it, but this time it was impossible to ignore. Somebody was tampering with the cars after he washed them.

The natural suspect might be David, since he had previously been in charge. But David was a hard-worker and honest. In fact, it was David who had been the first to comment on the issue himself. He had seemed genuinely befuddled. It wasn't him. Another suspect was Burris. While Burris had been nice initially, relations between them had soured. Burris had become aloof. Cheyenne and Tommie had taken a liking to him in the months he had been working here, so it could be jealousy on Burris's part. It was obvious to everyone he had a much stronger relationship with the kids than Burris ever had. Then there was the fact that, because he was honest, he ran his errands and trips to the warehouse much faster than Burris. What everyone had always known but had pretended not to notice had become apparent. Burris had been sand-bagging for years. If Burris was mad, he understood why. If Yui was going to pay them all anyway, and working hard would expose those who didn't work hard, one might argue it was in bad taste to work hard. But he wasn't doing what he was in order to expose anyone at the house who wasn't working hard. He simply wanted to work hard, because it helped with the boredom, and so long as he was going to be putting in the hours, he wanted to be busy. And in any case, one might always turn the argument back on Burris and others. If they expected him to be lazy in order to accommodate their desires, why shouldn't they be expected to allow him to work hard in order to accommodate his? Finally, there was Theresa. He doubted she would be the one to do it herself. But she might be the one asking Burris or whomever it was to do so.

He was staring at the cars, mulling over the mystery spots, when Michelle came up to him. "Yui wants to talk to you," she said.

"Okay."

He went upstairs.

"What's going on with the cars?"

He was glad she'd brought it up. "I actually don't know."

"You need to wash them harder."

"No, that's not it. I'm washing them the way I always had. It's only getting worse for some reason, but I haven't changed anything."

"What are you using?"

"Same supplies as always. The ones David had been using for years."

"Well, you need to figure it out. The cars look terrible."

"Okay." He looked at Theresa, who was pretending to be busy, flipping through some family photo albums.

"Oh, Yui, look at this one. This is a nice one," Theresa said pointing to a picture. Yui and Theresa started talking, and when it was clear Yui was done with him, he left the room without saying anything. He walked back out to the cars.

Michelle was still there.

"You'll need this."

"What's this?" He grabbed the clipboard and read the sheet. "A mileage log?"

"Yep."

"What for?"

"Yui's concerned that we're using too much gas. She thinks the drivers are using the cars when they're out for things besides work errands." Of course, the implication was that he was the one doing so. Michelle knew he wasn't, that it was Burris and the others, but she also knew that he already knew that too. There was no point mentioning it, since in any case, Yui had her favorites.

"Ugh, this is so absurd. They have so much money, and they're penny-pinching over gas. It costs more to fuel the plane one time for a trip to France than it does all the cars for the year."

"I know." The family got the SUVs straight from the plant for free. Every ten thousand miles, they would turn it in for a new one.

"Okay, whatever," he said. He helped Michelle distribute the clipboards so that each car had one.

"I've told Burris and Jane, too." Jane was a driver they'd hired two months ago for Ella and errands.

"Okay." He had an errand to run, so he got in the car, started the engine, and filled out the sheet, by putting down his name, the date, and the time. When he returned, he'd record the number of miles just driven, and the odometer.

That weekend, the time came to wash the cars. He grabbed the supplies out of the supply shed and got to work. As he was washing down the second one, Yui came out to him. She must have been watching him from inside, and wanted to take a closer look. He could see her confusion when she saw that his technique was impeccable. He didn't say anything. He had learned that most people are either clueless or sinister. If they're clueless, there's no point in trying to tell them what's really going on, since it will fly over their heads, and they'll think the one telling them the truth is speaking nonsense. If they're sinister, well, they'll just play dumb. Yui was clueless. He could see she would never understand that somebody at the house had been sabotaging the wash jobs. Then again, that assumed the culprit really did work at the house. Perhaps it wasn't Burris or Theresa or anyone else here. It could be anyone. After all the shenanigans he'd seen in Oxford, he knew anything was possible.

"Glad you're now paying attention to detail," Yui said. The implication was that he hadn't been before, but he didn't say anything.

She looked at the car as she spoke, "I want to ask you to take Cheyenne to church on Sundays. David has been driving her, but I have him taking care of something else now. Can you do it?"

"Yeah, sure."

"Okay, well, she leaves in fifteen minutes."

"Okay, I'll wash the cars when I'm back."

"I've told Kevin you're coming. He'll want to meet you. You remember him?"

"Yeah, the old family friend, the youth pastor," he said.

On the ride over, Cheyenne was in good spirits.

"I really love it here," she said.

"What's the sermon on today?"

"Something about the story of Joseph, I think."

"I see. That's a good story."

"You know it?"

"Indeed, I do," he said.

"Mom said you should meet Kevin."

"Yeah, she said that. He's the Youth Pastor?"

"Yeah, our family's known him forever."

They pulled into the parking lot and got out. A man in his early thirties approached them and turned to Cheyenne.

"Hey, Cheyenne! How are you doing?" Overly syrupy, he thought. The guy was a phony. The man turned to him.

"I'm Kevin," the pastor said.

He gave his name and extended his hand.

"You're free to join us today. We'd love to have you," Kevin said.

"No, thanks. I have work to do. I'll be back to get you when the service is over," he said to Cheyenne.

"Okay, thanks," she said. Kevin put his arm on her back, and walked her away. He got in the car and sat in the driver seat for a while. He hadn't meant to be rude, but he had no need to sit around and listen to a little homily about Joseph. He knew about betrayal. He knew about exile. He was living out the truth of the Scriptures every day in his life. The story of Joseph wasn't for him, as it was for others, just an object of curiosity once a week for an hour. He sighed.

The phone rang.

"Hello?"

"Where are you? You're supposed to be washing the cars."

"No, Theresa. Yui asked me to drive Cheyenne to church. I'm going to wash the cars when I'm back."

"Well, come back and ask for some errands when you wait."

"Okay, but by the time I get to the house, I'll basically have to turn around again to come get Cheyenne."

"Don't be lazy."

"It's not about that. The gas."

"What about the gas?"

"I thought we were supposed to scale back our consumption. Coming back to the house now is just needless miles."

"Don't worry about that. Come back," she said.

"Okay."

At the house, he parked the SUV and returned to washing the cars.

"What are you doing?" He looked to see Yui.

"Washing the cars."

"No, I mean, why are you back?"

"I thought I'd do something when I wait on Cheyenne."

"But what about the gas? You're going to have to head back again in a second. That's an extra trip!"

"Yeah, I know. I asked Theresa about that. She told me to come back anyway. I mentioned the gas, but she said not to worry about it." He could see Yui's mind drift off as soon as she knew she was going to be forced to hear that Theresa was responsible for what she was criticizing him for. A few seconds after he finished explaining, she turned to him.

"Well, you better get Cheyenne now. Make sure to log the miles."

"Okay," he said.

TEN

NOTHING happened that week. It was now Sunday, and it was time to wash the cars once again. There was more excitement in the air than usual at the house, because the family was gearing up for another big trip, this one to Turks and Caicos. The good news is that with the family gone, he could attend to his tasks without drama from the assistants, who would be gone. Yui ran a skeleton crew of drivers and workmen during vacations. The thought of coming into work without Theresa brought a smile to his face, as he was hosing down one of the SUVs. Even better, Alison had told him that Stuart and Linda were about to depart for six weeks to Italy. Carlos and Lydia, and some of the other extended family, would be going too. Neither of them could go, of course, since they had work, and in any case, he was relieved he didn't have to go. He could tell Alison was sad, because even though she didn't want to take a trip with her family, which always exhausted her, she did want to take one somewhere with him. That wasn't possible at the moment, however. As he began thinking about a section of the book that had been giving him trouble, he was interrupted by yelling.

"What have you been doing?"

"What?"

"Go upstairs right now! Yui has to talk to you. She's angry."

"Okay."

He found Yui lying in bed with a sleep mask.

"What's going on with the gas logs?"

"What do you mean?"

"You didn't sign them this week." It was true that he had missed a few entries over the course of the week's errands. Thus far, he'd been the only one logging any miles at all. There weren't any signatures from Jane or Burris or David.

"I'm sorry. It slipped my mind a few times. I thought we weren't doing that anymore, anyway," he said.

She took off her mask and looked at him carefully. "What are you talking about?"

"Nobody else is signing," he said.

Theresa interjected, "This isn't about others. It's about you. You didn't sign!"

He sighed. It was like being in an academic meeting with Quiller. Use the secondary literature, and there's not enough primary sources. Use the primary sources, and there's not enough secondary literature. No matter what one did, Quiller would criticize it. It was the same here. Sign the sheets, and he got no credit for it, even though he was the only one doing it. Don't sign the sheet, then suddenly he was in trouble for not signing, even though nobody else was signing, either. He pictured Quiller in his red sweater standing here in Yui's room, with a walkie-talkie in hand and a headset on, screaming at him about the gas sheets, or the mulch bags, or some heirloom stuffed away somewhere in the warehouse. He smiled.

"Is something funny?" Theresa asked.

"I was just thinking how you'd do great at Oxford," he said. Theresa and the others knew he was an intellectual or something, so she stopped, flattered by what she thought was a compliment that fed her pride.

"Really?"

"Oh, yeah, definitely."

Yui looked at him. "You can go now. Make sure you're signing the sheets. I'll have Regina talk to the other drivers." He turned to leave.

"Oh, one more thing."

"Yes?"

"Burris called. He's not coming in today. I need you to take the van to the dump. We're trying to get rid of some things before the trip, and we need the van emptied to make room for the luggage."

"Okay." In anticipation of Cheyenne now driving herself more frequently, one of his other new tasks had become trash duty. They were many recycling and trash bins. He had been helping one of the old gardeners, Nelson, on trash days. As a joke, at home, Alison and him had started referring to himself as "Dr. Basura." After all, he now had the DPhil. If it was easy to forget that he did, it was because nothing had really changed, which was precisely what he'd always expected would be the case. He was still a professional pariah, his family and friends still ignored the blackballing, and he really seemed nowhere closer to moving past his tarnished reputation than before. It was exactly as he had thought it would be. Carrell, Quiller, Klaus and the others had simply regrouped, ceding the thesis, but doubling-down on the blackballing.

His mind drifted to the viva in New York City. The viva itself had been uneventful. It lasted about forty-five minutes. He had a good discussion with the examiners, and after a brief consultation, they informed him that he'd passed. The internal examiner based in New York took him out that night for a dinner at a local Italian restaurant. It was a kind gesture, and they had a good time, but it only reinforced the oddity of his situation. No family, no friends, no supervisor there. Just the two of them. He didn't bother mentioning anything about the job he was working in Texas. He didn't mention the book, either. They'd spent a good portion of the conversation talking about Pelagius, possibly one of the most misunderstood men in history, in his opinion, he had told the examiner. The man's name had become synonymous with heresy, despite having by all accounts been an incredibly holy and righteous man. In addition to the job and the book, nor for that matter did he mention the fact that Andy, his old best friend, was currently somewhere in New York City ignoring him. He'd texted Andy in advance of the trip, saying he was in town for the viva, but he never had received a reply. How much had changed so drastically and quickly, he thought. Just a few years before, he had been in the city for a conference. He'd stayed with Andy. They'd spent the night out drinking. He'd taken a shower and changed his clothes in the morning, but he went to the conference still half-drunk. He cringed at the memory. As for the wedding, it felt like it belonged to a different lifetime. Maybe in a way, it did. As he was eating dinner with his examiner, he thought how strange it was, that now that he was sober and had passed an Oxford viva, his old best friend was acting like they had never even known one another. He bet Pelagius had known moments like that, he had thought.

Here in the room, he looked at Yui. "Where's the dump?"

Theresa gave him the address. He went out, and checked the van, which was low on gas. He signed the sheet, left the estate, filled up the van at Costco, and then drove out to the dump. It was out in a rural stretch of land, in a part within the city limits to which he'd never been. Once inside the facility, he drove for a mile along a dirt road that began slowly winding up a hill. At the top of the hill was the landfill. There were a few other trucks there, but otherwise things were still. He hopped out of the van, opened the back, and began unloading all the things Yui wanted tossed out. It was hard work, and soon he was sweating. He grabbed some water from the front seat and swigged it down. The place stunk, which made sense, as it was a dump, after all. It had a pungent sweetness about it, something redolent of what he'd heard of death. When he was finished unloading the van, he walked to where there was a view. Sunday morning in Texas at the city dump, tossing away old junk from an eccentric billionaire. The life of Dr. Basura, he chuckled.

Paul's words came to him, and he took a special delight knowing that they were words he could actually say he now truly understood, "Yea doubtless, I count all things but loss for the excellency of the knowledge of Christ Jesus my Lord, for whom I have suffered the loss of all things, and do count them but dung, that I may win Christ." The people he knew wouldn't believe him, but he'd never felt freer.

Eleven

A LISON was at work, and today he was off since Yui hadn't sent him any errands from the island, which meant he was alone at the apartment. The family had extended the trip, so rather than the originally planned two weeks, they had now been gone for nearly a month and a half. The family's departure had come at a good time for him. It had allowed him to make substantial progress on the manuscript. He was sitting at his desk with the window open for the breeze. The windchimes were tinkling softly. There were no hummingbirds, but the butterflies were out. He'd read a considerable chunk of the Levinas which was good. As for the book, it was coming along beautifully. When he'd signed the contract in Oxford, he had been worried that the timetable was too aggressive. But once he'd gotten into the swing of the writing, the chapters had unfurled one by one easily. He was over halfway done, and would have the full manuscript to the publisher by Christmas, just as he had intended. He thought about how a cigarette now would be nice, but instead he walked to the couch, patted Myshkin and Umi, and walked out the door. It was hot and humid, but sometimes a midday walk in the heat stirred his thoughts, or at least cleared his mind of extraneous ones.

He took one of his typical routes. On the lane, his mind turned to what he had seen. Or more specifically, his mind turned to what he had seen in light of the conversation he'd once had with Manan in Oxford. Manan had told him that the three temptations in a man's life were power, money, and sex. God had shown him the apex of power at Oxford, and he had seen it was nothing to be desired. God had now shown him incredible fortune with the family, and he had seen it was nothing to be desired, either. That left sex, he supposed. If he ever did see what the world considered to be the zenith of that, he was sure he'd be just as underwhelmed with it as he had been seeing power and money.

When he got home to the apartment, he didn't feel like going in yet. He didn't really have anywhere to be, but he felt like he did. He looked up at the clouds, and sighed gently. Then he realized it might be worthwhile to head to campus. There were some books he'd been meaning to get at the library, chief among them the Pelagius. He'd heard Pelagius had written a commentary on Romans. And there was an old Cambridge historian who'd written a book on the dispute between Pelagius and Augustine. He wanted to learn more about that, since that great theological dispute was shaping up to be relevant to the book's conclusion he would write. He walked a few blocks over into Midtown, and grabbed a seat on the transit car. Ten minutes later, he got off at the stop across the street from campus. He took a seat on a bench and stared at the park. The library wasn't closing any time soon, so he wasn't in a hurry.

Some joggers and cyclists passed him, and then there was nobody. He sat on the bench for an hour. As he was thinking about leaving, an old homeless black man approached. He had a scraggly beard, and torn clothing. Unlike so many of the homeless who showed signs of substance abuse, he didn't. The whites of his eyes were white as snow, without the faintest discoloration. He didn't smell of alcohol, and although he smelled like smoke from cigarettes, he wasn't a crack or meth smoker. The man walked up to him.

"Hey, brother, how are you?"

"I'm good. How are you?"

"Listen, I'm sorry to ask you, but I need your help."

"It's okay. What do you need?"

"I need some money for a shelter and a bus ride."

"Okay. I don't have any cash on me now. But I could get some."

The man's eyes lit up with gratitude. "Oh, thank you."

"You're welcome." He pointed across the street to the campus. "I was planning to go over there to use the library. There's an ATM machine there I know. Want to come with me?"

The man hesitated. "Well, you know, I don't like the people over there very much. They're evil."

He laughed. "Oh, I know. If you want to wait here, that's fine. I could come back to you."

The man looked across to the campus, then looked at him. "No, I'll be okay. I'll come with you."

The man stuck out his hand, "I'm Michael." He gave Michael his name.

"So what are you doing out here?"

"My boss is out of town, so I don't have work today. Thought I'd come over to campus to get some books."

"You read a lot?"

"I do."

"You?"

"Oh, yeah. Mostly the Bible."

"Me too," he said.

"Is that so?" the man chuckled. Then the man spoke, "*The wicked flee when no one pursueth—*"

He completed the verse, "*But the righteous are as bold as a lion.*"

"Oh, boy, sonny, you do know your Scripture," the man said humming.

"Proverbs 28:1, one of my favorite verses," he said smiling. "Come on, let's go to the ATM."

The man stood motionless for a moment gazing at him. "Your family."

"Yeah?"

"Your family. They hate you because of your heart."

He looked at Michael, "I know." They laughed, and walked across the street. They walked down the oak lane, crossed the grass, and passed through the main quad. They found the building on the other side of the hedges, and went to the ATM. He took out twenty dollars, walked outside, and gave him the bill.

"Is that enough? I can get more."

"No, that's plenty fine. Thank you," Michael said.

"You're welcome," he said.

"You going back to the transit?"

"No, I think I'll go to the library."

"You be blessed," the man said.

"You too," he said. They shook hands and went their separate ways.

He walked across the grass. He thought about entering the campus coffee shop where he used to meet Carrell, but instead he went straight for the rear entrance to the library. As he was approaching the door, he saw a figure in his peripheral vision approaching.

"Hey," the voice said. He turned to see Stuart.

"Hi," he said. He stood where he was, and Stuart walked up to him. His father-in-law was grinning.

"What you doing here?"

"Using the library. I'm here to get some books. Pelagius probably."

Stuart was quiet for a second, "How's Carrell?"

The fact that Stuart would ask that right now could have led him to say many things. To begin with, the timing of the question was egregious, to say the least. This was the first time in years that Stuart had ever asked him such a question. Stuart certainly had never cared to know such things when he was nearly being run out of Oxford. Nor had he cared during any number of the family visits since returning from Oxford. In fact, Alison had repeatedly pleaded with Stuart to talk to them about what had happened in Oxford, yet Stuart was refusing. When he'd been officially awarded the DPhil in May, Stuart and Linda hadn't said a single word about the accomplishment. It was like what had happened in Oxford, and what was continuing to unfold in its aftermath, never had happened. That Stuart would ask such a question now made perfect sense, given recent developments with Carrell.

After securing the DPhil, he had written to Carrell about having the meeting Carrell had mentioned. In writing Carrell, he took the opportunity to bring up the state of the book manuscript. If Carrell was willing to read the draft and offer any feedback, he'd be most appreciative, he'd said. The response he received from Carrell was diametrically opposed to what Carrell had said previously, though he wasn't surprised at the about face. The mask was now off. All the previous rhetoric about Oxford being evil and the people there having unfair animus towards his work was replaced with defensiveness of those very people. In fact, Carrell was now openly accusing him of having been the source of the turmoil. The words from Carrell's email entered his mind, as he stood here looking at Stuart.

> Nobody wants to help an iconoclast bent on driving the money-changers from the temple . . .
> Go find your own team . . .
> You think society is satanic . . .

At the time, he'd let the comment about society being satanic go unaddressed. There was no point in arguing with Carrell about that. He did, however, decide it had been time to address the issue of working with others. He brought up the volume Maureen had supposedly invited him to co-edit in Oxford. He asked Carrell what had happened to it. The moment Carrell had been waiting for had finally arrived. The email was dripping with venom. Carrell had sent over a list of the volume's contributors. On the list was Klaus. Of course, seeing this was supposed to drive him over the edge. Rather than responding angrily, as Carrell had anticipated, he simply wished Maureen and him good luck on finishing the volume. Carrell, though, was not finished,

"I personally approved every name on that list," Carrell had said.

So, there it was, just as he had surmised while still in Oxford. Carrell and Klaus, and perhaps Quiller too, had told Maureen to invite him to the volume. The invitation had never been sincere. He had patiently waited on Maureen, and when it was clear that he was not going to write to her to complain, they had told her to disappear. When it was clear to everyone that he'd been cut from the volume but didn't care, Carrell had ramped up the provocations. It had become comical, frankly. A few weeks before, for instance, he'd received an email out of the blue from a man named Todd Marshall. Marshall introduced himself as someone familiar with Carrell's work, and somebody who knew Maureen. He would be in town for a short visit to see Carrell for dinner, and wanted to grab breakfast with him as well. He knew the entire thing was a trap, but he accepted Marshall's breakfast invitation anyway. At breakfast, Marshall mentioned the dinner at Carrell's house the night before. They were talking about a volume Maureen was putting together, Marshall explained. Marshall pretended that he did not yet know he knew about the volume too, and he had kept quiet, letting Marshall play on.

"I'm very excited about the volume," Marshall said. "Maureen has asked me to co-edit it," he said beaming.

"That's wonderful. Congratulations," he said over his eggs. He didn't mention that Maureen had once invited him outside Tom Gate, or that he knew Carrell had told Marshall last night to bring up the volume here over breakfast. When Marshall saw that he wasn't going to be able to provoke an outburst, the visitor quickly finished breakfast, and that was it. He never heard from Marshall again. Carrell's having Marshall flit into his life had been a nice touch, had been a new low for his old supervisor, he had thought. When the breakfast hadn't provoked him as they had hoped, he knew they must have been angry. It only made sense, then, that a few weeks later, Carrell himself would finally here take off the mask in email correspondence. Carrell was relishing the fact that he had cut him from the volume, replacing him with Marshall. But the truly delicious part for them all was Carrell's inclusion of Klaus in the volume. It was a particularly sick move, given what Carrell knew Klaus had done in Oxford. Carrell had seen the lawyers' letter from Patrick and Dave. Carrell had also seen the letter Alison had filed as part of the academic appeal to the Proctors.

> When my husband received his acceptance to the University of Oxford, we were overjoyed. Though our relationship was very new, and accepting this offer would mean a year apart, we both readily agreed that going to Oxford would be the best decision. It had always been his dream to study here and we thought that the education and experiences he would receive here would be invaluable to him in his study of Philosophy. Our expectations of Oxford could not have been further from the reality of studying here and had we known then what we know now, we would have run screaming in the opposite direction! The unbelievable systematic and sustained abuse that we have endured over the past two years has been extremely harmful in a multitude of ways to us both . . .
>
> The stress caused by the egregious harassment my husband (and I by proxy) endured from the Faculty of Philosophy, Christ Church and the University as a whole, put me in a very precarious position health wise and meant I had to be admitted to the hospital. Although I do not blame the University of Oxford for my pre-existing condition, I do hold them partially responsible for the relapse that occurred during my time here.
>
> Furthermore, because of the stress that my husband was undergoing as a result of the University's actions, he was rendered unable to provide me with the kind of support that he otherwise would have been able to. As he was constantly at his breaking point due to harassment from members of the University, and the refusal of anyone to hold those accountable responsible and offer him aid of any sort, he had limited resources left to focus on my life-threatening illness. Oxford University stole this precious time from us and has left me, my health (mental and physical), and my life itself in a perilous position. If, God forbid, this illness ever claims my life, I want those at the University of Oxford who have been abusing my husband and I for the past two years to know that they are in part to blame.

Carrell knew that Klaus was one of the instigators behind everything Alison had described. Carrell had read her letter at the time, and he had followed all the details closely. Carrell knew the toll the events in Oxford had taken on him, on Alison, and on his dad. And yet, here now was Carrell still smugly working with Klaus, all as a way of taunting him. Alison's letter had continued,

Another source of harm has been the slanderous allegations about my husband by Christ Church students and faculty in the newspaper. I have always been, and still am, deeply proud of my husband and the kind of man he is. To have these false statements made in such a public manner and to have had my husband made a spectacle of has been deeply humiliating. The man I love is not homophobic or hateful and to have scores of people saying that he is has wounded me deeply as it also indirectly speaks to my character—what kind of woman would love and marry such a man? I have even been scared to say my name in public for fear that I might be wrongly judged or harassed as well. I'm terrified he might somehow come across this news article and have his opinion altered of us. It was deeply and shockingly irresponsible of the students, the Christ Church faculty, and the newspaper to print such false words and characterizations.

However, these sorts of despicable actions are what we have sadly come to expect from a University that seems to be devoid of any moral conscience, character, or integrity. The only solace Steven and I have is knowing that despite the best efforts of many of those at the University, we are able to escape this warped place, whereas they are unable to escape this terror, since the darkness resides in their hearts.

Not only had Carrell known all this about Klaus and Quiller. More importantly, Stuart and Linda had known it, too. It was bad enough for an old supervisor of his to look the other way to what had happened in Oxford, only then to turn around and work with the very people responsible. That made Carrell a snake. But there weren't words to describe what Stuart was doing. To allow this to be done to his own daughter was inconceivable. And now here was Stuart in the flesh, right after Carrell had revealed himself as being in cahoots with Klaus, asking him how Carrell was doing. He and his dad had always been right. They were all in it together. Even Linda knew everything.

Earlier this summer, in an email to his dad about the situation, he'd laid out what he thought was to come over the next few months as he worked to complete the book manuscript.

"I don't know what they're going to do," his dad had said. "They're trapped. It's so obvious that Stuart and Carrell got caught working with Klaus."

"I know," he had said.

"Do you think Carrell will have to retire in shame when everyone finds out what he allowed to be done to you and Alison?"

"Maybe. Everyone he works with are freaks though too, so he probably won't be ashamed at work. They will all just be angry that Carrell got caught and made it obvious. Really, there's no reason for him to retire anyway. His life is a big scam already as it is. He sits around and teaches the same class he's been teaching for twenty years once a week. The rest of the time he's busy drinking, fornicating, and golfing." Carrell, as it happened, had a membership at the same country club as Stuart and Linda and Yui's family.

In the later email exchange wherein Carrell had unveiled his collaboration with Klaus for Maureen and Marshall's volume, Carrell had made an even bolder move. Quoting directly the words from the email note that he had sent to his dad, Carrell acknowledged the network.

"As you surmised correctly, I'm busy drinking, fornicating, and golfing." When he had received the note from Carrell, he couldn't believe Carrell would actually be that obvious. He'd told his dad what Carrell had said.

"Yeah, he has access to technical assets. Or, his handlers do. Not surprised he'd taunt you like that. He puffed up," his dad had said.

Alison could not deny the bizarreness of it. Somehow her husband's former supervisor had access to what her husband had told her father-in-law in an email. Alison, who had been campaigning for her dad finally to discuss the Oxford situation, had raised the issue with Linda, thinking it would be the smoking gun that would force her parents to talk about the problem.

"Mom, it's really weird. How can Carrell have known that?"

Linda had stared straight ahead and pretended not to hear anything. After a few more unsuccessful attempts at trying to force Linda to explain how Carrell had known how her son-in-law had said how Carrell spends his free time, Alison had given up. And here now was Stuart, in his face on campus outside the library, flaunting the fact that he and Linda knew all about Carrell and Klaus and Maureen's volume. He sighed.

"I don't know, Stuart. I'm sure Carrell's fine. Maybe you should ask him," he said.

Stuart was quiet.

"We're back from Italy. Linda has a gift for you. I'll have her give it to Alison the next time Alison is over at the house," Stuart said.

"Thanks," he said. "I need to go to the library now. See you around," he said.

He walked away. He could see Stuart smirking at him through the reflection of the glass doors. Good, he thought to himself. With the DPhil in hand and the manuscript nearly completed, the network was feeling the pressure. If they wanted to become more overtly nasty and expose themselves, that was fine. This, he thought, was the contradiction at the heart of evil. Or, at least, one of the contradictions. On the one hand, evil thrived by operating in darkness. It delighted itself by lurking in the shadows. On the other hand, evil loved to dominate and humiliate others. The trouble arose for it when one withstood its provocations and taunts, since the degree to which it had to go to attempt to incite a response only increased. Over time, the provocations became so obvious that evil was forced to expose itself openly, which in turn weakened it, since the exposure deprived it of the darkness that was essential to its continuation. That was what was happening here. He was simply drawing Stuart and Carrell out of the darkness, and there was nothing they could do about it. He welcomed their provocations.

He opened the library door. Before walking in, he felt God had told him it was time speak. He turned around to face Stuart, who was still staring at him.

"You know Stuart, you are going to be judged for what you're doing," he said.

Stuart scoffed, "I don't believe in judgment."

He turned around and walked inside. The Pelagius was waiting.

He later got off at the Midtown transit stop, and walked home. At the gate, he decided to check the mail. Beneath the coupons and bills was a letter addressed to him. He grabbed it and looked. A letter from Paris, from 25 Rue de Petit Musc. It was a letter from one of the philosophers about whose work he was writing in the book. He made his way to the chair outside his apartment, and opened it, reading as quickly as his French would allow. The letter had been written with a type writer, though it was addressed and signed by hand in black ink. A note from Jean-Louis, he thought. He shook his head incredulously. Someone in Paris must have told the philosopher about his book, and now they were in touch. He knew what to do. He sat down at his desk, and drafted a reply letter. He didn't have a printer at the house, but that was no problem. He walked over to the nearby copy shop, sat down at a computer stall, and printed out his chapter on the philosopher. He walked home, and placed the letter and the book chapter in an envelope. The Post Office was closed already, so he would mail it first thing tomorrow.

TWELVE

T HAT night, Alison came home later than usual. She looked
tired. There was concern etched on her face. She sat down on
the couch with him and pet Umi distractedly.

"What's the matter?"

"Oh, nothing. I came back from my parents' house. They're back
from Italy," she said.

"I know," he said. She almost asked him how he knew, but she said
nothing. There was a pause.

"They got you something." She handed him a fine leather Italian
wallet.

He smiled. "Tell them I say thank you," he said.

More worry draped over her face.

"What is it?"

"Nothing," she said.

"Have you asked your dad about the lawyers' letter? You know I
want to talk to him about it," he said.

Alison sighed. "He doesn't understand," she said.

"Doesn't understand? What do you mean?"

"The letter. He doesn't understand it."

"Huh?"

She sighed exasperatedly. "I asked my mom. She said she has shown
him the letter. He can't understand what it says," she said.

"What do you mean? He can't read English?"

She got very quiet and somber. Tears were welling up in her eyes.
"No, no that's not it."

"What then?"

"He's dying," she said. He broke into laughter.

"It's not funny! I know you two don't get along, but it's not funny," she said.

"I'm not laughing because he's dying. I'm laughing because that's preposterous. He's not dying," he said.

"Yes, he is! My mom told me. I saw him today." He didn't mention that he had seen Stuart today, too, on campus.

"What's he dying from?"

"It's some neurological condition. They don't know what it is yet," she said.

"So now he suddenly has some mysterious neurological condition that just so happens to mean he can't understand the lawyers' letter? Unbelievable," he said, shaking his head.

"You think they'd make up something like that?"

"If he can't read and understand the letter, how's he at work?"

Alison was grief stricken. "That's the problem. He's already slipping. Mom says he's been noticing problems at work. He's forgetting things. He's not as sharp as he used to be. It's hard for him. He's going to have to retire soon," she said.

He sighed. "Okay, well, what? Your mom can't understand the letter, either? She went to Harvard Law. Have her come over, and I'll read the letter to them and explain it."

"Don't be absurd," she said. "This isn't funny."

"I know it's not. I'm being tortured by them. Carrell too," he said.

"What are you talking about?"

"I saw your dad outside the library today. When he saw me, he asked me how Carrell was doing."

"So?"

He dropped his head and stared at the floor. There was nothing more he could do. He realized that God was for some reason blinding her to the truth. No matter how much she saw, she didn't see. He would just have to wait for God to let her see what was going on. He thought on Abraham. This was a spiritual trial. Abraham couldn't speak, and neither could he. He would have to be misunderstood.

"Never mind, forget about it."

"Don't be angry at me. This is hard. I'm going to miss him," she said as her voice began to tremble.

"He'll be around. He's not dying," he said.

"I don't want to argue about it," she said.

"Neither do I." He stood up and went to his desk and grabbed the letter from Paris.

"Look at this," he said, handing it to her.

She looked at it. "Wow, this is amazing. What does it say?"

"It says that he's aware of my book. He told me about a book he's currently writing, and he said that if I'm ever in Paris, he would like to meet me."

"That's amazing! What are you going to do?"

He walked over and retrieved his papers.

"I have a note here for him. I'm going to send him the book chapter tomorrow. If I have the guys in Paris read their chapters, that will help me push the manuscript through the publisher. Quiller and Klaus and Carrell are going to try to sink the book in peer review. This will counter that. The publisher can't can the book with anonymous reviewers, when the very figures I'm writing about in the book have written and approved their chapters."

"Can you get a hold of them?"

"Yes, the others have email. Jean-Louis was actually going to be the hardest one to reach. He's notoriously private. He has no email. See how the note is written with a typewriter?"

"Jean-Louis," she said. "He's a little bug man," she said smiling.

"Yeah, he's a gem. I've read so many of his books," he said pointing to the shelf.

They were quiet for a little while.

"I think we should schedule a trip to Paris. It will be good for me to meet them in person," he said. "Can you get time off from work?"

"Probably, if you give me enough notice."

"Okay, well it won't be until sometime next year, after I've submitted the manuscript to the publisher."

"Okay," she said. She smiled, "Another trip to Paris!" He pictured all the birds at the Seine. It would be good to be back for a visit, he thought.

He smiled, "I think it would be good for us," he said.

"Me too," she said.

"I should get to bed early. I want to wake up early tomorrow, and start the week off with a good start. This is my last week of writing without having to worry about the job. The family's coming back to town next weekend. I'll have to get them at the airport, and I'm sure Yui will be frantic with things to do the second she lands, so it's going to be busy."

When Saturday came, he drove over to the estate, clocked in, got in the van, filled out the gas sheet, and departed for the airport. He had a number of things on his mind. For one, the papers to Jean-Louis had not made it to Paris. He had placed tracking on the package, and according to the USPS site, the package was in a recurring loop between Chicago and here. He had contacted the USPS about it, and they said that they were unable to retrieve it from circulation. It appeared the package would continue its circuit indefinitely. Rather than attempt to set the original package back on its proper course, he would ship everything again on Monday, this time with UPS.

He pulled up to the hangar. The men from before were there. The plane was taxiing to the tarmac. A few minutes later, the pilots cut the engine, and the family came down the stairs. They appeared to be arguing about something. They split into two SUVs, one driven by David, the other by Jane, and left for the house. He stayed behind and waited till the men had loaded the luggage into the van.

"All set, buddy," a workman said.

"Great, thanks. Take care," he said.

"You too."

On the highway, he hit traffic. The phone rang.

"Where are you?"

"I'm on my way, Theresa."

"You're taking too long. Yui needs you here. There's a lot to catch up on," she said.

"I'm sorry. I was waiting for the guys to load the van. Now I'm in traffic," he said.

"You always have excuses." There was silence on the line, as he heard Theresa talking to someone in the room.

"Yui wants to know where the shirt is," she said.

"The shirt?"

"Yes, the shirt. Yui handed you a shirt before take-off. Where is it?" He couldn't believe it. Six weeks later, after a trip to Turks and Caicos, and Yui was still worried about where a stray shirt had ended up.

"I don't know. I left it in the SUV. I haven't touched it."

"Well, everyone has looked for it everywhere. We can't find it. You need to find it."

"Why me?"

"Because you had it."

"No. I left it in the car. If it's not there, that means somebody has moved it. Whoever moved it needs to find it," he countered.

"Don't argue with Ms Yui." The phone clicked dead. Welcome back, he thought. The family had been here for only an hour, and Yui already had him on a treasure hunt for a six-dollar shirt that somebody had hidden on him. He hoped it was one of those assignments that eventually disappeared, but because Theresa was involved, he knew it wouldn't. She would continue egging Yui on to find it. He sighed.

He pulled up to the house at dusk. It was bustling as before, the workmen and assistants scrambling around the grounds.

Casey was waiting outside to supervise the workmen unloading the luggage from the van.

She looked at him with a wry smile. "How've you been?"

"Fine. It's great to have them back," he said laughing.

"Tell me about it," she said. Casey had been one of the assistants to accompany them to the island. "If you think it's bad here, you should see them on vacation," she said, shaking her head.

He looked at her, "Did they even use the quesadillas?"

Casey laughed, "I think Tommie may have had a couple the first day they were there."

"What was that all about?" he asked.

"No idea," Casey said. They laughed.

"I think I'm going to be quitting soon," she said. "I can't do this anymore."

"Yeah, I may too. I don't know if I can go through another Christmas season here."

"I know, it's awful. Christmas is the worst time for the assistants. It's probably even worse for you guys, since you have to do all the driving and lifting."

Theresa came out the side door and glowered.

"What are you doing?"

Casey interceded, "I was just talking to him about errands. He got back from the airport. Javier, Jorge, David, and Juan are unloading. Ask Yui who she wants to help unpack the bags." Theresa looked at them, and almost said something about how Casey wasn't in charge of her, but she went back inside without saying anything.

"I can't stand her," Casey said. "Neither can Michelle. Michelle might quit, too. Theresa's a lifer, it seems. She's probably aiming to take Regina's spot when Regina dies, you know, move into the house. Whatever," she said.

The side door opened again, but it wasn't Theresa. David was taking Bear out for a bath. He lost control of the leash in the doorway. Bear barreled towards them. He knew not to flinch or run. There was nowhere to go, anyway. Bear careened into Casey, knocking her down from behind. He started snapping at him, biting his fingers. Bear was barking, and David's yelling didn't help. "Bear! Bear! Stop! Stop it, Bear!"

The others unloading the van froze in panic. Eventually, they came over to shoo Bear away to the guest house, where David could corral him and put him back on the leash.

The men gathered around Casey and him.

Javier and Jorge were checking her for bites.

Juan turned to him, "You okay?"

"Yeah, I think so."

"Oh, man, look at him," Jorge said pointing. He looked down and saw his jeans were torn on the thigh. He felt something dripping down his leg.

"Oh, no, you're bleeding," Casey said.

The men walked over and examined the hole.

Javier looked up at him. "You have a bad bite. It's bleeding. You should go to the ER," he said.

"I'll be fine. Let me go tell Yui I've been bitten," he said.

He walked inside and found the lawyer standing in the kitchen. Evidently, she'd been waiting to come over to the house for a visit when the family returned from Turks and Caicos.

"Hi," she said.

"Hi," he said. "Well, I guess it's timely that you should be here."

"What do you mean?"

"I was going to tell Yui myself, but I guess I'll tell you as well." He walked over. She saw the tear in his jeans and the blood.

"Oh my, gosh," she said. "Bear?"

"Yes, Bear," he said. "Listen, I have no intention of suing. I just thought you should know you're lucky he did this to me, rather than somebody who would. He's a dangerous dog. He could seriously hurt someone," he said.

David came into the kitchen.

"I'm so sorry. I didn't mean it," David said.

"It's okay, David, I know," he said.

"Let me see. How bad is it?" He took a look. "You might need stitches," he said.

"It's fine."

David turned to the lawyer. "You need to get rid of Bear. This isn't the first time he's bitten somebody." Hearing what David said, he looked at the lawyer, whose face flushed red with embarrassment. So, he wasn't the first victim, he realized. That meant the lawyer and Yui didn't care if Bear bit the workers. They probably figured most people who worked here wouldn't have the resources to sue, and even if they did, whatever they claimed was pennies to the family. The occasional lawsuit from a wronged employee was simply a business expense for them, he saw. He wanted to clear his head. Ordinarily, he would wash the cars on Sunday, but he decided he would start washing now.

He started with Tommie's SUV. As he was hosing it off, Tommie came down out front.

"I saw you washing from inside," Tommie said.

"Yeah," he said. "How was the trip?"

"Oh, you know," he said. They both chuckled.

"Listen, I need a ride to dinner. Steak house again. David offered to drive, but I want you to drive." He stopped hosing.

"Oh, yeah, sure. When do you need to go?"

"Half hour," he said.

"Okay. I'll finish with yours, and I'll be ready. I'll meet you out here."

"Cool, thanks," Tommie said. "Let me get changed."

An hour later, Tommie came down to the car in dress pants and a white collared shirt.

"Let's roll," he said.

"Sounds good. Which restaurant?"

"Truth BBQ," he said.

"Truth it is," he said. They climbed into the SUV and drove off. On the road, they were quiet for a few minutes until Tommie turned to him.

"I looked you up over in Turks," Tommie said.

"Yeah?"

"Yeah. You were in Oxford?"

"Yeah."

"What are you doing out here?"

"Long story," he said laughing.

"I have time," he said.

"You ever heard of Jacob Rothschild?"

"Yeah, I know who he is."

"He went to my college."

"I see. So, you have powerful enemies," he said.

"Well, they certainly think they're powerful," he said laughing. "In the grand scheme of things, they are nothing, though. Christ is King, not them," he said.

"What did you see over at Oxford?"

"Enough to know what people hear is true," he said.

Tommie was quiet. "All that occult stuff?"

"Yeah," he said. "It's not just limited to Oxford. It's a network."

"Yeah, I know about that with the Catholic Church. The whole Mystery Babylon thing," Tommie said.

"You know a lot more about this stuff than most people," he said.

"Well, I did my research," he said. "I've been thinking about going back to church. Cheyenne wants me to go. I told her I'd go tomorrow. Could you drive us?"

"Yeah, sure. What time?"

"Nine-thirty," Tommie said.

"Then I shall see you both at nine-thirty tomorrow morning," he said as they pulled up to Truth.

Tommie got out of the car.

"Tommie?"

"Yeah?"

"I know you already know this, but I wanted you to hear it."

"Yeah?"

"These guys inside you're going to meet."

"Yeah?"

"They're not really your friends. True friends will never lead you into sin," he said.

"I know," Tommie said.

"Look at me as an example. All the guys I thought were my friends, guys I'd known for years, guys at my wedding, they've all disappeared on me. They don't like me anymore because I don't party like I used to."

Tommie stared up at the sky, looked at the restaurant, then looked at him. "Thanks, man," he said.

"You're welcome. Don't worry, you'll figure it out." He watched Tommie walk into the BBQ. That night on the couch, he felt like what he had said might have meant something. There was no way really to know. He patted Myshkin on the head, and then went to bed.

THIRTEEN

IT was now September, which meant summer was fading. The manuscript was nearing completion. Even better, he had heard from Jean-Louis. The philosopher had read the chapter on his work, and thought well of it. There were some minor suggestions he made, but that was it. That was not the only development. In addition to being in touch with Jean-Louis over his chapter, he had also heard from Claude, Victor, Jean-Luc, and Pierre. All four had read their respective chapters, and been impressed. Claude had even sent a number of his other books as a token of gratitude. Having the philosophers in Paris aware of the book was imperative. Their positive feedback on the manuscript would help him push it through the publisher's peer review. He had asked whether they might wish to endorse the book, and they had said yes. He'd written the publisher to provide an update, and his editor had said he'd be in touch with them to get their endorsements.

When he pulled up to the house, he saw a car he had not recognized before.

He asked David, who was vacuuming it. "What's that?"

"Mary Anne's home for a visit," he said.

"Mary Anne?"

"Yeah, the eldest daughter. She's at Vanderbilt," David said. When Angela and the lawyer had interviewed him, they must not have mentioned Mary Anne, since she was away at college.

"I see," he said.

David got a look on his face. He looked around to make sure nobody else was in the yard

"What is it?"

"Listen, uh, well, they want me to run an errand," he fumbled.

"Who?"

"The girls."

"Okay."

"They want to go lingerie shopping at Victoria's Secret," he said.

"Oh."

"I'm old. I don't want to be there. Can you do it?" Of course, he felt the same way. He didn't want to go, either. The fact that he was closer in age to the girls might even make it more uncomfortable.

"Yeah, I guess so. Why can't Mary Anne just drive them? Her car's right here," he said.

David shook his head. "I know. I tried talking to Yui, but she won't have it. She's worried that they'll have an accident. She wants one of us to drive," he said

"Okay. Where did the car come from? She didn't drive all the way from Nashville, did she?"

"No, we took it out of storage," he said.

"So Yui had you take Mary Anne's car out of storage, but now she won't let Mary Anne use it?"

"It's Yui," he said laughing. "It's not supposed to make sense."

Just as he was about to walk into the house, the girls came outside.

David pointed out at him, "He'll be driving you," he said. The girls looked at him.

He stuck out his hand and gave his name to Mary Anne.

"Hi, I'm Mary Anne," she said.

"How long are you here?"

"Just a week. School starts soon."

"Yes, I heard. Vanderbilt?"

"Yeah."

"That's a good school."

Cheyenne interjected, "I want to go there also. I'm hoping to get in," she said.

"That would be nice if you could go there together," he said.

Ella rolled her eyes, "Can we go now?"

"Be quiet, Ella. Don't be rude," Mary Anne said. "Sorry," Mary Anne said.

"It's fine. Let's go." The four of them got into the SUV, the girls in the back, and him in the front alone.

"Which location?"

"The one on Westheimer," Cheyenne said.

"Okay." When they arrived, he parked across the street. "I'll wait for you here," he said.

"Thanks," Mary Anne said. The three girls got out of the car and walked into the store. He sighed. The errand was pushing the threshold of what he could accept. If Mary Anne wanted lingerie, that was fine, he thought. He disagreed with the morality of it, since Mary Anne wasn't married, but at least she was in college. The other two, though, were still underage. He didn't know if it was better or worse that they were doing the shopping with the oldest sister, and evidently with the full approval of their mother too. He wondered how the dad would feel about it. Knowing the way things were these days, the dad was probably a womanizer, with many mistresses. He would be in no position to tell his own daughters not to become like the very girls they saw him value.

When they were almost to the house, he looked into the rearview mirror.

"I have a question,"

"Yeah?" said Cheyenne.

"Your dad. Does he know you're shopping at Victoria's Secret?"

Ella rolled her eyes, "It's not a big deal. Why do you care? You're just the driver," she said.

"Don't be rude," Mary Anne snapped. She looked at him, "Yeah, he knows. He's friends with the owner."

"Of the store we were just at?"

"No, the company."

Cheyenne turned to Mary Anne, "Dad knows the owner of Victoria's Secret?"

"Yeah, Grandpop and Dad used to go on camping and fishing trips with him. He came to the house one time when you were very little. His name's Les," she said. "Grandpop knew him from college in Ohio."

"I don't remember meeting him," Cheyenne said.

He looked into the rearview at Cheyenne, and pulled through the gate into the estate. He would make it through this Christmas, submit the book manuscript to the publisher, and then quit the job.

FOURTEEN

HE took a bite of his frozen yogurt. Alison had gone inside for a napkin, and would be out in a second. Summer had ended, and the first couple months of fall had brought something of a routine. The book manuscript was now finished, though he hadn't yet told anyone. Things at work hadn't changed much. It was errands, and washing the cars. In a few weeks, Yui would begin preparations for Christmas. He'd been taking Cheyenne and Tommie to church on Sundays. Tomorrow he would be taking them again.

"Do you need a napkin, Koala?"

"No thanks, Barnacle," he said.

"How's the book coming? You haven't mentioned it in a while."

He leaned back in his seat and smiled, "It's done."

"It's done? When? You never told me!"

"I finished it earlier this week. I wanted to make sure it was really finished before I told anyone."

"What? That's amazing! We have to celebrate!"

"We are. Frozen yogurt with my bug," he said. She smiled.

"When are you going to submit it to the publisher?"

"I'm not sure. I can at any point."

"What's the next step?"

"There will be a peer review. It should be fine. All the guys in Paris have seen their chapters, so nobody can really argue."

"Yeah, that's so important," she said. "Have you heard from Jean-Louis?"

"Yeah, we've been talking. He has a new book coming out. Well, it's an older book, but it's going to be out in English," he said.

"That's exciting."

"Yeah, he's so prolific," he said.

"Does he still want to see you in Paris?"

"Yeah, he says he wants to meet you too."

Alison was startled. "Me? Why?"

"Because he knows how important you are to me. If I'm going to be there, it makes sense he would want to meet you too," he said.

"I don't want to see him. He won't like me," she said.

"Of course, he'll like you. Why wouldn't he like you?"

"I don't know. I'll think about it."

"Trust me. You won't regret meeting him. It's a very special opportunity."

"When are we going?"

"I'm thinking in the spring. I have to talk to the publisher first and figure out some things," he said.

"Okay, well let me know what dates you're thinking when you know," she said.

"Okay."

She smiled, "Woo hoo! Your book is coming out!"

"We'll see," he said.

"What do you mean?"

"Well, they don't have it advertised yet. And there's no talk of galleys."

"Galleys?"

"The author copies they send in advance of the publication."

"But you haven't submitted the manuscript yet."

"I know, but the point is that they're not even laying out a publishing schedule or anything. They're keeping me in the dark," he said.

"I'm sure it's fine. They asked you to write the book," she said. He didn't mention how the contract had probably been a sham from the beginning.

When they got home, he went to his desk. "I have to send something," he said.

"What?"

"A message to the editor at the publisher," he said.

"Okay," she said.

He drafted a short note saying that he was enclosing the completed manuscript. He mentioned also that Claude, Pierre, and Victor had all committed to providing endorsements. He gave the editor their contact information. He clicked the send button, and exhaled.

"It's done," he said. Well, not really, he thought, but it was close enough.

A week passed without a response from the publisher. He wasn't surprised. Alison, though, could sense his agitation.

"What's wrong?"

"Still haven't heard from the publisher," he said.

"I'm sure they're busy. They're probably contacting the guys in Paris first," she said.

He looked at the time. "I have to go right now, or I'll be late. I'm taking Cheyenne and Tommie to church this morning," he said. They kissed, and he left.

He dropped them off at the church, and then sat in the parking lot. Everyone at the house was busy with a yard project, and they had the supplies they needed for now, so it was unlikely any of the assistants would be contacting him with errands to run. He opened his Bible, and did some reading. After a little while, his phone buzzed with a text message from Cheyenne. She told him to come out to the parking lot when the service was over. Kevin wanted to see him. He sighed.

When the service ended and people started entering the parking lot, he opened the door and stepped out. Tommie, Cheyenne, Kevin, and a girl he'd not seen before were walking over.

He shook Kevin's hand. "Hi."

"Hi," Kevin said.

Apparently, Cheyenne had brought Kevin out in order to introduce her friend to him in front of Kevin.

Cheyenne turned to her friend, "This is Rebecca," she said. "We're friends from school, and she's been coming to church." He remembered the Rebecca from a few years ago, the one who had sent her friend to spy on him at the bar. He shook his head thinking about it, glad that those days were behind him.

He stuck out his hand. "Hi, Rebecca," he said.

Rebecca shook his hand and smiled. She turned to Cheyenne, "Who's he?"

"He's the driver," Cheyenne said smiling.

Tommie said, "He fights bad guys."

Rebecca looked at Tommie confusedly, "What?"

Kevin cleared his throat. "Well, good to see you. I have to get back to the office," he said. Before going, Kevin hugged Cheyenne, "Bye."

When Kevin left, Cheyenne turned to him, "Can Rebecca come with us?"

"Yeah, sure. Does your mom know?"

"She won't mind," Cheyenne said.

"Okay," he smiled.

Rebecca looked at Cheyenne, then looked at him. "I think Cheyenne has a crush on you," she said laughing.

He looked at Rebecca. "No, it's not like that. Come on, let's go," he said.

They all climbed in the car and drove to the house. When he got to the gate, Regina was waiting on the intercom. "It's good you're back. Yui has said we're starting Christmas decorations today," she said.

Rebecca turned to Cheyenne. "Christmas decorations? It's not even Thanksgiving yet," she said.

Tommie answered, "That's just how our mom is," he said.

He pulled up and parked the car. Down the driveway, he could see that Yui had the workmen setting up the triage looking tent where they'd sort through the boxes he and the other drivers would be bringing back from the warehouse. He had been expecting a couple more weeks before this would begin. He sighed.

He heard footsteps behind him. "Sighing again?"

It was Yui and Theresa.

"You have such a bad attitude," Yui said. "You're my laziest worker." Theresa smiled widely.

"Go join the others and get to work. We're going to need you to head to the warehouse soon," Theresa said.

"Go on, you heard Theresa," Yui said.

He had done his best. There was nothing left here to accomplish. He felt it was time. The workers in the driveway had stopped working. Yui had been speaking loudly, and they knew she was close to an outburst. A few seconds later, Michelle and Casey came outside with Enrique. Everyone was there.

He looked directly at Yui. "Listen, Yui, this is absurd. Your kids need you. I just got back from driving Cheyenne and Tommie to church. You should be there with them. They don't need all these Christmas decorations. Last year you left without even enjoying them, anyway. You should get rid of all of us, send us all home, and take care of your family."

Yui went ballistic.

"You stupid little brat. How dare you talk to me about my family! What do you know? You're just some stupid driver! Do you know what everyone thinks about you here? They all hate you! They hate you! Everyone thinks you're weird and laughs about you behind your back. You're a loser. Don't ever question my parenting. You're fired!" she shrieked.

"I was already intending to quit," he said calmly.

She walked up to him and reached for his shirt.

"I'm going to drag you out of here myself. Get off my property! Get out of my house! I'm going to call the cops!" The others had gathered in a group and were watching silently. A few of the workmen walked over to calm Yui down.

He began walking down the driveway to the gate. Yui followed right behind him, yelling at him every step of the way.

"Boy, your wife must be really lucky to have you for a husband! Loser! Freak! Writing some book? Nobody cares! Get out of my house! Don't ever question my family again!" As he neared the gate, he could feel her trail off behind him. One of the workers had grabbed her, and asked her to come inside. She was sobbing. After walking through the gate, he turned around.

Michelle, Casey, Javier, Jorge, and David were at the gate. Some of them were on the brink of tears.

Michelle spoke, "We're so sorry. We don't think what Yui said. We don't think that," she said.

Jorge looked at him, "I'm sorry."

"Sorry," Javier said.

"It's okay, guys. Good luck," he said quietly. He nodded his head, and turned around to leave. Alison had dropped him off, which meant he didn't have the car. He could call for a ride, but he decided he'd walk instead. It was a few miles, but he had nowhere else to be. He wasn't angry, just sad. He would miss the kids. But there was nothing more for him to do. He fought back tears on the way home. When he got there, Alison was gone, so he lied down on the couch and closed his eyes. His phone was ringing incessantly from Theresa and Yui. He didn't answer, and after a while, he fell asleep.

FIFTEEN

B
Y Christmas, he knew for certain the fix was in at the publisher. The editor had written to say that he'd been in touch with the philosophers in Paris, in order to receive their endorsements. This would have been extraordinary had it actually been true. Unfortunately, it was a lie. He'd written them all in Paris, and they'd said that they'd never received anything from the publisher. It was baffling in a way. It made little sense for the editor to lie like that when it was sure to be discovered. He'd had the same thought, of course, when he had caught Klaus lying about the DGS back in Oxford. The reality, however, is that desperate people did desperate things. And that was the situation here. The manuscript had made it immeasurably farther than anyone had ever anticipated that it would, and it is was now in stronger position than ever. Not only did he have the DPhil from Oxford, but he had the philosophers in Paris now openly supporting the book. The prospect of sinking the manuscript during peer review was no longer viable. Nobody could bribe him, and nobody could blackmail him, either. That left only force.

He knew to most people it would sound absurd. Alison, for one, didn't believe he was in any physical danger. This was partly because she couldn't imagine someone having the requisite mindset for a book such as his to be a genuine motive for murder. But he knew that for the people with whom he was dealing, it very well could be. The public could view an episode of *Morse*, or *Lewis*, or *Endeavour*, and think it was an exaggerated portrayal of Oxford politics. Given his own personal experience there, he knew better, of course. The jealous dons he knew personally were not the sort above murder. They loved nothing more than their reputations, and they would do what was necessary to protect their careers. For them, social existence was the entirety of their experience, and for them, this meant their identity was in their job. A loss of professional reputation or standing would be equivalent to death. They were in a death struggle. Anything was possible from a group of unscrupulous people who thought they were facing extinction.

He called his dad.

"Hi, Son."

"Hi, Dad."

"Any update?"

"Not really. I just want to think out some things aloud."

"Go ahead."

"Okay, so the plan is to block the book by sinking it in peer review. But at this point they can't do that, since no anonymous referee has the credibility or authority to say work about the guys in Paris is inadequate when the guys in Paris have themselves said it's good."

"Correct," his dad said.

"Stuart and Linda are now caught, because if the book comes out, they won't have any excuse for how they've been trashing me behind my back, and lying about what really happened in Oxford. They know Stuart will be exposed for what he allowed to take place there."

"Correct," his dad said.

"Carrell's in trouble for the same reason. We have him tied directly now to Klaus in his own words. And it's even worse, because in addition to having a motive for letting Klaus and Quiller sabotage the thesis in Oxford, he's been caught fighting the work before when I was here originally in Texas. He's going to be the laughingstock of the profession when everyone finds out that he let me sit out here on a library card writing."

"Correct," his dad said.

"So what do you think they're going to do?"

His dad took a long breath. "They're running out of options, Son. You know what that means," he said.

"Yeah, I know. I just wanted to make sure we were on the same page."

"I love you."

"I love you too," he said.

"I have to go," his dad said.

"Wait. One more thing."

"Yeah?"

"Alison and I are going to take a trip to Paris in April. I need to meet the guys in Paris."

"Don't worry. I'll help you with it. You know it's my pleasure."

"Okay, thanks."

"Bye," his dad said.

"Bye," he said.

He walked into the apartment.

Alison looked up from the couch. "Who were you talking to?"

"My dad," he said.

"Oh," she said.

"He's going to pay for the Paris trip," he said.

"That's nice. Tell him I say thank you," she said.

They were quiet for a moment.

"You don't have to go."

"I know."

"You sure you can handle it?"

"I'll be fine."

"Okay, well she wants us there tomorrow at five. We'll stay for as little as possible. I promise."

"Okay."

The next evening, they pulled up to Stuart and Linda's. As they walked up to the house, the dog was barking.

"At least you have the dog to play with," Alison said.

They rang the bell, and Linda answered.

"Oh, sweetie! You made it!" She gave Alison a big smooch on the cheek, then looked at him.

"Hello," she said.

"Hi, Linda," he said.

They came inside and took a seat in the living room after putting the presents down.

"Where's Dad?"

"He's upstairs wrapping presents," Linda said.

"Dad wrapping presents? Dad never wraps presents," Alison said.

She smiled, "He decided he'd start a new family tradition this year."

A few minutes later, Stuart came sauntering down the stairs.

"Hi, Alison," he said. Stuart stared at him and nodded. Alison stood up to give her dad a hug. He sat where he was. Before he would have stood up to shake Stuart's hand, but at this point, after campus, he didn't care anymore.

They ate dinner, and then it was time for hot coco and presents. He could see that Linda and Stuart were getting excited.

Alison opened hers first. There was the customary exchange of thank you and you're welcome. Stuart and Linda opened their gifts next.

A week from now, he would not be able to remember what Alison and had gotten them. He could tell, though, that Stuart and Linda had taken special care to make sure to get him something they'd never forget. Let's see how they try to top the wallet from Italy, he thought, as he looked at his gift.

Linda looked at him, "You're not going to open your present?"

"Sorry." He began unwrapping it with everyone watching.

He undid the ribbon, opened the box, and pulled away the paper. "Ah, a sweater," he said, nodding knowingly.

"Show me!" Alison said.

He lifted it out of the box.

Alison started laughing. "Mom! Dad! That's the ugliest sweater I've ever seen! What were you two thinking?"

Stuart turned to her, "We heard they're popular in Oxford."

Linda looked at him, "Do you like it?"

"Thank you," he said.

"Try it on," Linda said.

"Mom, you know he's shy! He can try it on at home." He sighed. Alison was interpreting everything from within the domain of the "perhaps"—the realm, in short, where opening the gift from her parents only to find Quiller and Simpson's red sweater was nothing more than a coincidence. When they got home, he'd toss the sweater in the closet with the Italian wallet.

He looked at Alison and grabbed her hand. "I love you," he said.

"I love you too," she said. They kissed. Nothing else mattered.

SIXTEEN

I T was the new year, and tomorrow was the annual city marathon. One of Alison's childhood friends was running for charity, so Stuart and Linda were invited, and naturally they'd invited Alison and him along too. After the race would be a luncheon downtown.

"What's the name of the friend again?" he said as they parked the car.

"Molly," Alison said.

"And the mother?"

"Dorothy."

"Okay."

They found a spot at the finish line and waited. When the race was over, Alison received a phone call.

"My parents are in the finisher's tent with Dorothy and Molly. They said for us to meet them at the restaurant."

"Okay, I'll follow you," he said. They held hands, and walked a few blocks over. The restaurant was closed to the public. Alison mentioned they were here for the event, and knew Molly. They were taken to a white linen table.

A half hour later, the event was beginning to fill, and they heard excited voices walking towards the table. They stood to greet everyone. Alison and Molly hugged, and there were handshakes and hellos. Stuart took a seat at the head of the table, with Molly, Dorothy, and Alison to his left. Linda took a seat to Stuart's right, across from Alison and him. They scanned the menus, ordered drinks, and talked about the race and Dorothy's charity organization. After they had done all the catching up and Molly and Alison had gotten reacquainted, Dorothy looked at Alison and him.

"So, Linda has told me you two are very busy."

"Yeah," Alison said.

Dorothy looked at him, "You have a job in River Oaks washing cars?"

"No, not anymore. I quit," he said.

Linda interjected, "You quit?"

Alison spoke, "Mom, it's fine. They were being terrible to him there."

"Just like everyone in Oxford was too, right?" Stuart mumbled under his breath.

He looked at Stuart. "Did I hear you say something about Oxford? I hope so. I knew you'd eventually get around to it. It's only been two years, Stuart," he said.

"Now, now, don't be testy with Stuart," Linda said.

"Mom, he's not. We've been asking Dad to talk about it for years."

"Don't attack, Daddy," Linda said.

Dorothy attempted to get the conversation back on the rails. "Any plans for summer?"

Alison lit up. "Actually, yes! We're taking a trip to Paris."

Dorothy spoke, "Paris? Why's that?"

"Well, it's my favorite city," Alison said, "and he has colleagues there. His book is about to come out, so he has to meet people there who are going to be endorsing it," she said proudly.

The table got silent as Alison waited for Linda or Stuart to respond. Stuart stared into space and said nothing. After a painful silence, Molly brought up her race again, and the table went through the same conversation they'd had earlier in the lunch. As the meal was winding down, Linda turned to Molly and Dorothy.

"Did you hear the terrible story about First Baptist?"

"No," Molly said concernedly. His attention piqued. First Baptist was Cheyenne and Tommie's church. He didn't mention it. Instead, he would wait to see what Linda had to say.

"It's just so terrible," Linda said. "Before coming over here, we saw on the news that a youth pastor was arrested on child molestation charges. Apparently, he was abusing some of the kids at the church."

"Oh, heavens!" Dorothy said.

Alison went to speak, "Isn't that the same church that—". He squeezed her hand firmly under the table. She looked at him, and fell silent.

Linda continued, "There's no telling how many victims. The hope, of course, is that he was just a weird loner. But indications are that there were others. It may have been a ring," she said, sipping her iced tea. She took a bite of her Caesar salad and fell silent. He looked over at Stuart, who looked at him, and smirked.

When they left lunch and got into the car, Alison turned to him.

"Isn't that Cheyenne's church?"

"Yes."

"I'm going to look it up." She scrolled through her phone. "It says here the guy is—"

"Kevin."

"Yeah? How'd you know?"

"I've met him."

"Oh, but how'd you know it's him?"

"Good men know when they're dealing with a bad man. I could tell Kevin was a bad man. I'm not surprised he was the one."

"Are you going to call Cheyenne?"

"No."

"Why not?"

"What's there to say?"

"I hope nothing happened to her."

"Me too."

"I'm sorry."

"For what?"

"For how my parents ignore everything you're doing," she said.

"It's okay. You appreciate my work. That's all that matters," he said.

They drove the rest of the way home in silence.

SEVENTEEN

COLLOQUIALLY, Apocalypse meant the end. This was true, biblically also. Of course, it in that context also meant a revealing. For everyone who had been privy to the events over the last few years starting in Oxford, he knew their eyes were being opened. Things were self-evident. This was good, since it meant that even if he still couldn't speak about any of it, because people were still too scared to discuss it, he wasn't nearly as isolated as he had been before. At the same time, the manifestness of the situation meant that those who had been behind orchestrating it were now liable to become dangerous. There were a lot of people who had questions to answer and who weren't going to be able to answer them convincingly.

To begin with, there was Stuart, of course. A few days after the marathon luncheon, Alison had offered to write to Stuart in front of the rest of the family, demanding that he finally address the situation back in Oxford and everything it had left in its wake.

Speaking of him, Alison had written, "Dad, I think you owe him a conversation about everything." Naturally, Stuart had not replied, and nobody else in the family said a word about it. Stuart was allowed to do whatever he wanted, and Stuart knew it.

He was at his desk when Alison came up behind him to kiss him before going off to work. She could sense that he was deep in thought.

"Is something wrong?"

"No, not at all. I love you," he said.

"I love you too," she said. He turned around, and she looked at him worriedly. "Be safe," he said. She left the apartment.

He spun his chair around and looked out at the neighbor's yard. It was winter now, which meant the flowers were dead. The butterflies were gone, as were the hummingbirds. There were no rainbows, and the birds had flown off to warmer, sunnier climes than here. It had been thinking he'd been considering doing for a while. Today was the day. He walked over to his couch and looked at Myshkin.

"Hello, my little man," he said.

Myshkin started meowing. He patted his head, and Myshkin began doing his circles.

"What do you think? Should I go expose a bad guy, today?"

Myshkin meowed.

"Okay, I'll be back soon," he said.

He walked down to the local copy shop, took a seat at the computer station, and printed out the documents. There was the lawyers' letter from Dave and Patrick, the letter from Alison to the Proctors, the emails from the Junior Censor harassing him at the college, the emails from the DGS discussing how Klaus had been lying, the defamatory articles from the newspapers, the decision from the Senior Proctor voiding the first irregular viva, and the letter from Oxford notifying him of his DPhil being conferred. He put everything in a folder, and walked to campus. He knew where exactly to go, because he'd been there before.

He entered the Physics building and took the escalator. A receptionist was at the desk. He was clean shaved, and in a suit, his wedding suit, as it happened. The folder and his demeanor suggested he was here on business, and that it was serious.

The receptionist looked at him as he approached.

"Hello. I'm an alumnus of the university. My father-in-law, Stuart, works here in the department. I have some very important documents I've been meaning to discuss with him. It concerns a very serious family matter. Could you possibly accompany me to his office?"

"You don't know where his office is?"

"Oh, I certainly know it. The issue is that knowing Stuart, he's liable to lie, which means he very well may distort the nature of my visit if there's no witness. I think it would be to everyone's advantage that there be someone else there. That way Stuart will know not to bother trying to waste everyone's time with a lie."

"Oh, I see. Well, I guess I could do that," she said. The receptionist looked at the other, who nodded.

They walked together to the elevator. "He's up above."

In the elevator, the receptionist looked at him. "What's this about?"

"I'm not going to tell you, because I don't want you to vomit. For now, out of respect for my wife, I'm not going to discuss what her dad has been doing."

The receptionist looked down at the elevator floor. When the door opened, they began walking down the hall to the corner office. They could see the door was closed.

"It looks like he's not there," she said.

"Oh, no, he's in there. He's hiding. Trust me," he said.

She looked at him and said nothing.

As they got closer, she spoke again, "I really don't think he's in there. We should go."

"What? We're not going to knock? Let's knock and see what he does," he said. He walked to the door and knocked on it three times. There was silence. He knocked three more times.

"Stuart?"

There was silence.

"See, he's not in there," she said.

"I'm not sure about that. He's a coward, so he's probably hiding. He's been caught lying." He held up the folder. "I'll leave this all here for him." He would have slid the documents under the door, but there was no gap, so he rested them up against the office door.

"That'll do."

As they were walking down the hall and had nearly reached the elevator, they heard the office door open. They turned around.

Stuart stuck his head out of the office, looked left, looked right, looked down, looked up, grabbed the documents, and closed the door. Stuart had stared right at them, but hadn't said a word.

"Told you," he said, looking at the receptionist. The receptionist hung her head.

In the elevator, they were quiet. The door opened to her floor, and she walked to the desk. He waved to her colleague. "We've now delivered the documents. There was some initial question as to whether or not my father-in-law was in his office. As it turns out, as I suspected, he was hiding. The good news is that he now has the documents. Many thanks for your assistance," he said.

Outside, he called his dad.

"Hello?"

"Hey Dad, I made a big move just now. I want you to know what's going on," he said.

"Okay, tell me."

"I just went to Stuart's office and left all the Oxford documents at his door."

"Oh, good. What did he say?"

"He hid from me."

"He hid from you? Not surprised," his dad said laughing.

"I had a receptionist accompany me so he can't make up a story," he said.

"Oh, good. How do you know he'll get the documents?"

"Well, I left them there at the door. But it's even better than that, we saw him grab them."

His dad started laughing. "Oh, this is so good. Little Howdy Doody caught. Let me guess, he opened the door, looked left, looked right, looked down, looked up, grabbed the documents, and then scurried into his office, right?"

"Dad, *exactly*," he said. He started laughing. "How'd you know?"

"It's Looney Tunes. Stuart's a cartoon villain. I knew what he would do."

They laughed some more.

His dad spoke, "So what's next?"

"We'll see how Linda and Stuart play it."

"Has Stuart answered Alison's email yet?"

"No, that's why I left the documents. I'm done playing games."

"Good. I'm so tired of this. I have had to sit around and watch everyone let this weirdo smirk in my face for years. I still can't believe the Skype call."

His memory turned to the event in question. It had been a few months before Alison and him left Oxford. The viva had been failed, the newspaper article had been printed, and the Junior Censor was on the attack. They'd just had the meeting at King's Bench with Patrick and Dave. Linda had scheduled a Skype call with Alison, to see how everything was going. When the time came, Alison and him had sat at the desk, with his dad sitting behind them on the edge of the bed.

"Hi, guys! How are you?" Linda had said waving.

"Hi Mom, hi Dad," Alison had said.

"Hi, Alison," Stuart had said.

There was a pause. "Hi, Scott," Linda had said to his dad.

"Hi Linda, hi Stuart," his dad said.

They talked about the weather for a few minutes. Then Linda addressed his dad.

"So how's your trip, Scott?" she had said, smiling. Stuart sat smirking.

"It's fine," his dad had said.

"Good," Linda said, turning her attention back to Alison.

A few minutes later, his dad stood up from the bed and walked into the living room. He couldn't take it anymore. Here he'd flown all the way from California, retained lawyers, and done everything he could to keep his son out of jail on a hate crime charge, try to right a sham viva, and to protect his daughter-in-law, and Stuart and Linda, who were both in a much better position to help than he was, were sitting there gaslighting him, pretending nothing was even happening, as if he'd on a whim decided to fly to Oxford. It was outrageous. At the time, he knew that if he walked away from the call also, Stuart and Linda would whisper about his dad and him. They would say his dad and him were being rude. They would ask whether Alison was okay there. They would insinuate that he was delusional, that nothing unusual or wrong was happening. They would say his dad was there for nothing, and that he was unnecessarily interfering with Alison's life. Anything they had to do to break up the marriage, they would do it. It had taken all his strength to sit through the call and not say anything. When they hung up, he walked into the living room and looked at his dad. "Let's take a walk."

When they got outside, his dad spoke, "These people are freaks. You think they don't know why I'm here? Of course, they do. Stuart could pick up his phone in his office and call someone here at Oxford and have this all fixed in five minutes."

"I know, Dad," he said.

"Did you see his little smirk?"

"I did, Dad." He stopped walking. His dad looked at him.

"Don't worry, Dad. It may take a while, but he won't be smirking one day. I promise. God will judge him."

When he got off the phone with his dad, he called Stuart.

"Hi Stuart, this is your son-in-law. I'm just calling to leave a record that your receptionist and I delivered a number of important documents to your office today. We saw you open the door and take them, so it's good to know you're in possession of them. As you know, Alison and I have been asking you to discuss a number of matters dating back a number of years now, and yet you've refused. I would love to understand why you've been refusing to do so. When you've had the chance to review the documents with Linda, please contact me at your earliest convenience so that we can schedule a meeting to have a family discussion about everything. Thanks."

That night, at the apartment, Alison came home from work. He was at his desk with Myshkin.

"How are my boys?" she said smiling.

"We're good."

She kissed him.

"Did you hear from your dad today?"

"No, why?"

"Just wondering." So, Linda and Stuart were still trying to concoct a story. It would be interesting to see how long it took them.

"Did you hear about Oxford?"

He turned to Alison. "What? No," he said.

"The Senior Proctor. He's dead."

"What?"

"Yeah, you know how I look up the local news stories back there sometimes?"

"Yeah."

"I saw an article. He died on Christmas Eve."

"How?"

"Car accident."

"Car accident?"

"Yeah."

"More like yeah right," he said, shaking his head in disbelief. He looked it up. Sure enough, it was all over the news, with obituaries in the *BBC*, *The Guardian*, and *The Telegraph*. The man who had overturned his irregular viva had, it seemed, been murdered. Well, he thought, many people wouldn't ever think so. They wouldn't come to suspect that even *perhaps* he'd been murdered. To them, it was another innocent, unfortunate auto accident. Of course, the death was a message to those who had a need to know. That included him. If the Senior Proctor was first, he might well be next. After the previous death threats and the attack on the High St and now this, it was clear the network was capable of coming for him, and would do so. He sighed. He'd left them no choice.

Eighteen

T HE next day, he had an email from Stuart. It was terse,
"Never contact me by phone, by email, or in person ever
again," it said.

He laughed. Having the receptionist there had been a good judgment call. It had prevented Stuart from crafting some fake story about him supposedly charging up to the office unannounced in a threatening manner. It would have been the same nonsense narrative that had been planted in the Oxford newspaper about him. Since Stuart couldn't deflect from the documents anymore, Linda must have told him to hide. At this point, they would increase the intensity of whatever lies they had already been spreading. Knowing them, they might start openly attempting to call into question his sanity. After everything they had been caught doing, the only way for them to defend themselves was to destroy his credibility.

He went outside.

"Hey, neighbor."

He looked down into the courtyard. "Oh, hey, Trevor," he said.

"Listen, I'm leaving on a trip again for a few days. Could you take care of Kyle?"

"Yeah, sure."

"Great, I'll leave the keys under the mat. I'll walk him now. If you could, take him out again tonight."

"Will do," he said. "Have a good trip."

"Thanks."

He went inside to do some reading. He thought about reading some Merton, or maybe Pascal, but ultimately, he settled on some Kierkegaard. He was still reading when Alison came home.

"There's my little author," she said.

"How was your day?"

"Good."

"Yours?"

"Fine. Trevor's leaving. We're watching Kyle."

"Okay."

"I'm going to take him for a walk later. Want to come?"

"No, I'm pretty tired. I'm going to shower and head to bed."

"Okay." He could tell that she'd read the email from Stuart to him. She had no way of explaining why her dad was refusing so vehemently to discuss the documents. He felt bad for her, since he understood it must be hard to see that her dad was hiding something. He wouldn't bring the issue up now. It could wait.

He woke up groggy on the couch after having dozed off while reading. He checked his phone. Past midnight, he saw. He was about to walk to the bedroom, when he realized he'd forgotten to walk Kyle. He opened the door, locked the apartment, and went downstairs. Kyle was barking at the door. He grabbed the key from under the mat, opened the door, put the leash on Kyle, and walked onto the street.

"Come on, this way," he said tugging at Kyle's leash. They walked down Emerson away from Midtown. The lamplight reminded him of the streetlight from his first place in Oxford. The walk, he decided, would give him a chance to think. The trip to Paris was slated for April. Alison had gotten the time off from work, they'd booked the flights, and found a place to stay. Jean-Louis had confirmed he'd be in Paris. The philosopher had given him his phone number, and told him to call it when he made it to Paris. They would meet in person. The others had also agreed to see him. It would be a busy trip, but by the end of it, he would have the manuscript in a great position. The publisher might even contact the guys in Paris and get the endorsements before he even left for Paris. But if the publisher didn't do so, he'd always be able still to secure the endorsements himself in person. He hadn't yet received a publication date or production schedule. The manuscript was still presumably undergoing peer review, so while the timetable was tight, he should have time to get to Paris before the book was sent out for production. He'd already selected the cover image, a beautiful painting he'd seen at the Musee d'Orsay during one of their previous visits to Paris.

Something down the street caught his attention, interrupting his ruminations. He was approaching a t-intersection, and a few houses off down the street on the right, was a parked SUV. He had walked the neighborhood countless times and never seen it. It felt like it might be there waiting for him. He made a left at the intersection, and began walking down the street away from the SUV.

"Come on Kyle," he said, tugging the dog from a bush. He surveyed the surroundings. Most of the house lights were out. Nobody was out walking. He heard the engine of the SUV come on, and he turned around to see the headlights flick on. The driver floored it, and the SUV came speeding by them, and screeched to a stop a few houses in front of them across the street. He stopped. The SUV was idling outside a small apartment complex. Perhaps the driver was there to pick someone up. Perhaps the driver had been at the wrong address when he first saw the SUV, and the driver had turned the engine on and sped over because whoever was waiting for a ride told the driver he'd been waiting at the wrong spot. *Perhaps*, he thought, shaking his head. This was no time to make decisions based on what most people would think was perhaps the case. That kind of thinking led to mistakes, and in a situation such as this, he was beginning to think that meant getting himself killed.

He didn't move. He would watch the SUV, which was still idling with its lights on. He would not walk past it. The driver's window was down. It was raining. If he walked by, the driver could shoot him with a silenced weapon and drive off. He'd be dead, and nobody would know who'd done it. Yes, perhaps it was all nothing. Perhaps. But it wasn't worth making a mistake so potentially grave just because social norms dictated that he was being paranoid. Maybe in his last moments, the Senior Proctor had told himself that whatever was going on around him was really just nothing. And look at what had happened to him, he thought. *Das Man* said "one" should shrug off the feeling he was experiencing, and that he should ignore the feeling he was having that told him he shouldn't walk by the car. "It's probably nothing," one says. And the next thing one knew, one was dead. No, he would wait right here.

When a few more minutes passed, the driver must have realized he was not going to be budging. The SUV started to leave. If it gets to the stop sign and turns around, it will be time to run, he thought. At the stop sign, the SUV pulled into the street and began to make a U-turn. When it crossed back through the crosswalk, it began speeding. He tied Kyle's leash to a fence, and ran around the corner back down the street from where they'd come. The streetlamp was out, so it was dark. He positioned himself behind a thick oak. If the SUV makes a right and comes down the street, there's no doubting that he's being followed, he decided. The SUV turned right, and slowly came down the street. As it approached, he slowly edged against the trunk of the tree, moving clockwise, as the car approached. By the time it had passed him, he'd moved to the other side of the tree. He would wait here to see what the driver did next. At the intersection, the SUV turned right. He assumed the driver would think he wouldn't follow, so he walked down the street to the same intersection. When he reached it, he peered down the street to the right. The SUV was not there. Probably, the driver had gone up the next street or the one after it. He made a right at the intersection. Beside him was an apartment complex on the corner. He made a right at the street which he realized was probably a mistake. He'd forgotten that the street was exposed, with very few trees or bushes. If he were spotted here, there would be nowhere to hide. He walked down to the end of the street, where he reached the same t-intersection as before, only this time a block over from where he'd first spotted the SUV. He looked both ways and saw nothing. This, in retrospect, he would realize, is where he made another mistake. He should have gone left or right at the t-intersection, since the SUV must have made a left and would be heading down the street behind him. But instead, he turned around, and walked back down the street he'd just walked up which was leading him in the direction of the SUV. When he got back to the same corner apartment complex, the SUV was coming up the street on his right. There was nowhere to go. The porch light of the complex was on, and there were cars in the lot, which meant people were home. He looked around, but nobody was out walking. He stood behind a waist high brick wall at the entry. If necessary, he could duck behind it.

The SUV pulled up to the curb, and the man, who had his elbow already resting on the window, leaned all the way out. He had a smile.

"You live around here?"

"Yeah. You?"

The man said nothing. He realized he'd seen him before. It was the man Alison and him had seen in the parking lot outside the Chinese Consulate. This was the same SUV, too.

He waited for the man to speak.

"I'm looking for my dog. It's missing," he said. Nice touch, he thought. It was a plausible enough excuse for being in the neighborhood, and of course it was the driver's way of noting that the driver had seen him leave Kyle behind.

"I'm sorry."

"You haven't seen it?"

"No."

124

"Where do you live?"

"Over on Richmond," the driver said. Richmond was too far. There was no way anyone truly looking for a missing dog would have come this far.

"I see."

Before he had a chance to ask the driver for a description of the dog, the driver spoke, "Well I'm going to keep looking. Let me know if you find anything," he said smiling. He drove off toward Emerson, where he made a left, heading back toward the t-intersection where he'd originally seen the driver parked. He had to make a decision about which way to go. He turned around, and went back up the street he'd just come up. With any luck, the driver would assume he'd want to head straight for home, which would mean the driver would make a U-turn at the t-intersection and come back down Emerson to the intersection with the corner apartment. If the driver did that, he could get behind the SUV, and decide from afar which direction to take to get to the apartment without being spotted again. He reached the t-intersection. Kyle was still tied up where he'd left him. He took the leash, and led Kyle down Emerson toward the complex where he'd spoken to the driver.

Something told him this was not over, though, so he tied Kyle to a post and walked forward. A few places from the intersection, he heard the SUV revving behind him and screeching down the street. He began to cross the street, but within seconds, there was nowhere to go. The SUV hung a right, and cut him off in the sidewalk, almost running him over. He stopped. The SUV was parked a foot in front of him. He looked through the passenger side window, to see the driver had already exited the vehicle. The man was walking toward the trunk where'd he then come around to this side. This was really it, he thought. The man's going to shoot me. He darted to the front of the SUV, walking past the hood as the driver reached the trunk. A second later he heard the man come around the other side and curse when he wasn't there. He made a beeline through the intersection, where he could hear the driver come around the front of the SUV and start into the intersection behind him. In the heat of the moment, he'd failed to realize that if somebody had intercepted him like this out on the street, there could be others at the apartment. He had to get home to Alison.

When he had nearly crossed the street, he could feel the man behind him watching. There was no point in running. The man would simply get back in the SUV and follow him down the street. If the man didn't already know where they lived, which at this point was extremely unlikely, he couldn't lead the man to the apartment. He would make his stand here.

He turned around and strode back towards the man.

When he had been a boy, he had dreamed of being a combat hero. The accounts of battlefield bravery had captured his youthful imagination. It was the very mentality Andy's dad, Ken, had recognized so well, and done everything he could to dissuade Andy and him from. To Ken's credit, wars were shams. When he had read the stories of the Marines in WWII, he had imagined himself there, riding the landing craft into the beach, storming over the seawall, throwing grenades into the bunkers, holding his position in a foxhole against all odds. It was all foolish, he realized when he got older. But there was something about his childhood imaginations that now made sense to him. What had always excited his imagination, he now understood, was the question of whether or not he would be a coward, of whether or not, if placed in such a situation, he would be up to it. He had always thought he would be, but he had acknowledged to himself that probably nobody thought he would be a coward. So there was really no way to know. As he walked toward the man now, he realized he had an answer. He was not a coward. He was angry, but he had no bloodlust. He had no intention of hurting the man, which, of course, he knew he could not do unarmed anyway. But even if he had been armed, he would have had no desire to kill, not even in self-defense. There was nothing about this world worth killing another man over, he saw. He would rather lay down his life, than take one.

He had not expected things to end like this, so suddenly. One minute he had been out walking the neighbor's dog, and the next he was about to be staring down the barrel of a gun. He would die a martyr's death, only there would be no witnesses, and nobody would know. It would simply be considered a random act of violence. His dad would know what had really happened, but nobody would believe him, and his dad would have no way of proving it. He wished Alison would know the reason why he had died here. One day, he would tell her about it in the Kingdom. In the meantime, he hoped that she would move on, marry someone else, and have a family. He would miss her.

"What are you doing following me? Get out of here," he said to the man from the Consulate.

The man stood in the middle of the intersection, and said nothing. He lifted his jacket and flashed a handgun on his belt. Then the man reached for something, and pulled out his phone. The man pointed his phone camera at him, took some photos, and then got in the SUV and drove away without saying a word.

It had been the strangest experience of his life.

Being alive moments after thinking he should be dead was strange. He would never know for sure, but he believed the man had let him live, because he had respected how he'd responded. Of course, that alone wasn't sufficient to explain why he was alive. The man could still have shot him anyway. God had intervened. People would laugh if he said so, but it had been a miracle. Then again, the very same people who would laugh at his account of things were the types who had never faced a hit-man and lived. What they thought really didn't matter, since they weren't in the game, and if he had their mentality, his corpse would be lying next to Kyle up the street after having passed by the window when the SUV had been idling outside the small complex. It was better to trust God and his intuition than the ignorance of foolish men and their idle talk.

Kyle, he thought. He'd almost forgotten. He went down the street, grabbed the leash, and ran back to the house with the dog, opened the gate, put the dog away, unlocked the door to his apartment, and went inside.

"Honey?"

The lights were off, and it was dark. He barged into the bedroom and flipped on the switch. Umi and Myshkin were on the bed sleeping with Alison. He took a deep sigh, and leaned up against the bedroom wall.

Alison stirred in her sleep. "What's going on?"

"Somebody just tried to kill me," he said. He could tell she thought he was joking.

"No, I'm serious. It was like the Proctor that you read about in the paper. I should be dead right now. It was a miracle," he said. He waited for a response. She had fallen back to sleep.

He would tell her in the morning.

NINETEEN

THE next morning, he had a lot to think over after Alison had left for work. He had tried explaining what had happened the night before, but understandably she didn't know what to make of it. It was the sort of thing that was impossible to understand unless one had been there. He had thought about taking it to the police, but a number of reasons had persuaded him to do otherwise. In the first place, he knew that the only remaining danger to his book was the story getting around that he was some sort of loon or paranoid. Running off telling everyone about how he'd survived a hit was not conducive to avoiding that sort of narrative about him. In fact, there was a high likelihood that whoever may have ordered the hit assumed that, even if it failed and he survived, they would be able to use to their advantage his reaction to it, which was sure to give people the impression he was losing his mind. In addition, there was the problem that even if he went to the police, there was nothing for the police to go on. He didn't have the plate to the SUV, and his description of the driver would be too generic. Of course, that was why the bagman from the Consulate, who apparently was also a hitman, was so useful to whoever employed him. There were a million young white men with short hair like him. Finally, there was the further fact that, although it was more or less clear to him who might have had a hand in last night, he wasn't in a position to explain it to anyone else. While there were plenty of people who had a clear motive to have him killed, it all belonged to a shadow world that the public and the authorities pretended not to exist.

Take the driver. By the looks of it, his intuition told him the man had been a Marine. His thoughts turned to the film *Enemy of the State*. He'd seen it in theaters as a kid with his dad. When they'd left the movie, his dad had told him that he couldn't believe the number of classified projects the film had shown. Presumably, his dad had in mind things to do with the satellite technology and other surveillance assets. But in retrospect, there was much more. To begin with, the opening assassination of the Senator was a clear allusion to the Foster murder. But more interestingly, at least for him now, was the way the film had portrayed the black-ops team that ran the NSA operation. His mind turned to the scene when the NSA villain recruits some jarheads who were about to be canned from the military. As it happened, he'd read about how Marines were popular for such projects. There was a Marine base not far from here in Louisiana. That could be it. He laughed when he thought about the SUV from last night, which even matched exactly the SUV the Marines were driving in the film. If he tried to tell anybody about what had happened last night, most people would have no idea what to make it of at all, and of the few who did, they would associate it with a Hollywood film they'd seen. To them, it would sound as if he were simply lifting a plotline from a movie he'd once seen.

What the Bible partly meant by darkness was now clearer to him than ever. Spiritually, the concept was a metaphor for man's ignorance and blindness, among other things. He had seen this darkness for himself. For instance, it was this darkness that explained why, for now, there was no point in even attempting to explain anything about last night to anyone. People, he saw, lived in varying degrees of willful ignorance of the nature of reality and the world around them, especially the evil, and, frankly, they liked it that way. Beneath the smugly dismissive faces of those who scoffed at the idea that the sort of things that had happened to him last night really happen, were scared and defiant children trapped in adult bodies, people's whose clearest glimpse into how the world really worked would be relegated to the movies they watched, though of course they would never know that. For those still imprisoned in the cave, movies were only fantasy.

Even if he couldn't talk about it with anyone, it was still necessary for his own purposes to figure out, as best he could, what was really behind last night. His intuition was that it was tied to the Proctor's recent demise, which meant it was tied to the viva, which meant it was tied to the book. The publisher didn't want to put out the book but there was no way out of it, Quiller and Klaus and Carrell and many others didn't want to see it out, either, so somebody in the network had offered to take care of it by taking care of him. Of course, there was an argument for thinking this wasn't the case. For one thing, the man in the SUV had come from the Chinese Consulate. That suggested it was Stuart. Stuart, after all, was working with the Chinese government, and if his Chinese partners had found out that his son-in-law knew too much about how the research that Stuart was doing in the lab was being used for the CCP against America, they might have wanted him taken care of, so that Stuart's cover wasn't blown. Of course, Stuart had the further motive that he was now directly tied to everything that had also happened back in Oxford, since he had let it all unfold while playing dumb. In a way, it was unnecessary to figure out precisely who had done what, since when it came down to it, there were multiple people and institutions, all of whom had a shared interest in seeing him dead.

He walked over to his desk and sent an email to his editor, asking whether there was any update on the review of the book or word on the endorsements. It was as good a place as any other to start piecing together answers. If trees are known by their fruits, he would make others finally bear theirs, whether it be bad or good.

Twenty

THEY landed late in Paris. When they checked the time, he realized that he'd barely make it to his first appointment. He was due to meet Pierre for lunch at one-thirty. It would make a bad first impression to be late, so he must hurry. They got off the plane, and he went ahead to clear customs. Alison offered to take care of the luggage and meet him later at the place in Paris. He kissed her, said goodbye, and made his way to the train. When he got above ground at the Luxembourg stop, he was disoriented. He made his way toward where he had thought the university was, but he had guessed wrong. Soon he was lost without phone service. He tried asking some locals about how to find his destination, but his French was terrible. By the time he made it to the university, he was nearly an hour late. He trudged up the stairs, and found what looked like an empty department. He tried all the doors, and one opened. Inside was a stunned receptionist who had not been expecting a disoriented American to barge in.

He apologized profusely. He cleared his throat, "*Je recherche Pierre. Nous dejeunons—*"

"Ah, you must be the American," she said in perfect English. "Let me ring Pierre. He must be down at the café waiting for you." A few minutes later, Pierre came trudging up the stairwell, with an angry look on his face.

"Ah hah! There you are! Well, come on, let's go. I have a meeting I need to get to, but we have time for lunch," he said.

"I'm so sorry. Our plane was delayed and then I got lost—"

"Bah, don't worry about it." He smiled, "You're here!"

They wound through the streets until they made it to a café. When they walked in, everyone knew Pierre, including the waiter who greeted them, and evidently had been holding their table.

Pierre slapped him on the back, and introduced him to the waiter.

"*Bonjour*," he said.

"I hear you're coming from Texas," the waiter said.

"Yes."

"You're a cowboy?"

"No, originally I'm a Californian."

"Eh! Ah! A Californian. So, you're a surfer," the waiter laughed.

"No, no. Look at him! He's a movie star," Pierre laughed.

The waiter laughed, "Okay, enough with the jokes. You must be hungry! Please, have a seat, and enjoy."

They sat down outside, poured some water, and began talking about the book. By the end of lunch, it felt like Pierre and him were great friends.

"I can't wait to see the publication of the book," Pierre said. "Thank you for writing it," the Frenchman said.

"Well, it's been an honor to work on it. I'm hoping the book brings more attention to your work," he said.

The Frenchman smiled, "Well, me too!" he laughed.

There was a pause.

"Have you heard from the publisher yet?"

"The publisher?"

"Yes, my editor said he had contacted you about providing an endorsement."

Pierre's face frowned. "No, no. I haven't heard from anybody. What's his name?"

He gave him the name of the editor.

"No, I haven't heard from him." Pierre looked concerned. "When's the publication date?'

"They haven't said."

"They haven't said?"

"No."

"That's strange."

"Yes."

"You've submitted the manuscript?"

"Yes."

"When?"

"Last December."

"Four months ago, and still nothing?"

"Yes."

"Phew, that is very strange. Okay, I will send you the endorsement, and you send it to him. Deal?"

"Deal." They clinked glasses, finished lunch, and said their goodbyes.

Back at the place, Alison was waiting.

"How'd it go?"

"Great, Pierre's going to endorse it. He said he never heard from the publisher. I knew it."

"Why would your editor lie?"

"Long story. Doesn't matter at this point. This is why we had to come here. It eliminates all the mystery," he said.

"Yeah," she said.

"I need to call Jean-Louis," he said.

"Are you nervous?"

"Very."

"You'll do fine."

He rang the number. After a while, it went to voicemail, which was his worst nightmare. At the beep, he began leaving a very clumsy message in broken French. It wasn't pretty, but it conveyed the essential, that he was here, and the number at which he could be reached.

He hung up. He laughed.

"What is it?"

"It makes me feel like it's the nineties again, when you'd play telephone tag. The place here has a voicemail, but I'm worried I'll miss his call and won't figure it out. I should just sit here by the phone and wait," he said laughing. "There's no telling when he will call."

"Maybe we should go out. We could go to the Tuileries."

"Sure. I need to stop worrying. It'll work out," he said.

They got ready, and as they were about to leave, the phone began ringing.

"Go get it! Get it! It's ringing. It's probably him," Alison said excitedly.

He fumbled for the receiver and answered just before the call went to voicemail.

"*Bonjour*, hello?"

A very tender, trembling voice spoke in English just as bad as his French.

"Hello. This is Jean-Louis."

"Hello, Jean-Louis." He gave his name.

"You are in Paris?"

"Yes."

"Are you free tomorrow?"

"Yes."

"Do you know les Place des Vosges?"

He'd heard of it.

"Yes."

"Meet me there at the statue of Louis XIII at three."

"Okay. I will see you then."

"Good, bye!"

He hung up the phone.

"What did he say?"

"We're meeting him tomorrow somewhere called les Place des Vosges."

"That's just down the street! We've been there before! When?"

"He said three."

Alison paused. "We?"

"Yes, of course."

"Did he mention me?"

"No."

"Well, maybe I shouldn't go."

"He already said he wants to meet you. He didn't mention you because his English is poor and he was nervous, and he assumed you know to come anyway, since he'd already invited you."

"He was nervous?"

"Yes, I think so. Which is funny to me, because he's a very famous philosopher. He shouldn't be nervous. But that goes to show how humble and sweet a man he is."

"Okay, I'll go. I can't wait to meet him."

"Me too," he said.

The next day, they arrived early.

"Is that the statue?"

"Yeah, that's it," Alison said. She could tell he was nervous. She squeezed his hand. They walked over to the statue, and waited. They surveyed all the people in the park, looking to see whether any of them might be Jean-Louis. A few minutes later, a short man in a hat and suit wearing a backpack came strolling into the park.

"That's him, I think," Alison said.

"You think so?"

"Yeah," she said.

The man walked toward the statue, turning his head as he surveyed the park.

"It looks like he's looking for someone. He must be looking for us," he said.

When the man got close, he cocked his head, and smiled.

"*Bonjour, Je suis Jean-Louis,*" he said.

They walked over to him and shook his hand.

Jean-Louis assumed a very serious posture, put on a dignified face, and bowed to Alison. "In France," the philosopher said, "it is customary when meeting a woman to say *Enchanté*. I have never understood that. How can one be enchanted without knowing the person first?" They all laughed.

The three of them chatted the best they could, Jean-Louis in his broken English, they in their broken French.

"Well, I should leave you two to it," Alison said. "See you back at the place?"

"Yeah," he said.

"Okay, great, take your time," she said smiling.

Jean-Louis cleared his throat and looked at Alison. "Now that I have gotten to know you, *Enchanté mademoiselle,*" he said. She smiled, and she and Jean-Louis laughed.

"*Merci, monsieur,*" she said.

When Alison had left the park, the two of them turned to leave.

"Em, I, em, how do you say? I know a place, this way," he said. They crossed a number of places until they took a seat at a café on the Place de Bastille.

"Come here often?"

Jean-Louis laughed, "No, actually I don't. I usually don't go to cafes," he said. He was touched. Apparently, Jean-Louis was going out of his way to host him.

"Em, would you like something to drink?"

"Yes, I'll have a coffee. You?"

"Water," he said smiling. They sat in silence for a while, enjoying the scene, and each other's company. There was so much he would want to say if he knew French better, or if Jean-Louis knew English better. It could have been frustrating, but in a way, he began to feel that the language barrier between them was bringing about a powerful silence. Words were great, but sometimes they could be a hindrance to experiencing whatever escaped them, anyway.

Nonetheless, they periodically filled the silence, doing their best to communicate various things. They talked about theology and philosophy, and even the academic job market. From what he could gather, the market was as terrible here in Paris as it was back home. The philosopher lit a cigarette. The experience of smoking in Paris with the great philosopher, whom he now considered something of a friend after their exchange of letters, was tempting. After a few puffs, Jean-Louis began coughing violently. He thought about saying Jean-Louis might consider quitting, but he didn't want to be rude. The man must obviously know that he should. He smiled gently at Jean-Louis, who shook his head. "Stupid things," Jean-Louis said.

The philosopher put his backpack on the table and looked at him. "I have a gift for you," he said. He took out a book of his and handed it.

"Oh, wow, thank you," he said, opening the cover. Jean-Louis had signed and dated it. He turned the page over, and read a snippet, "... *dix brèves meditations* ... "

"I hope you like it," Jean-Louis said.

"Thank you so much. I'll be sure to read it," he said.

After a while, it was time to go. They stood from their chairs, and began walking back the way they had come. Suddenly, Jean-Louis got a great big smile on his face.

"Come this way. You must see something." The man who was in his late sixties, sprung to youth, and jogged down the street. He stopped. "There's a canal beneath us. Look," he said pointing. The water rushed beneath them. He thought he saw Jean-Louis' point. Beneath us is an incessant river, the waters of eternal life. He smiled, and Jean-Louis grinned.

The Frenchman looked at him searchingly. "*Vois-tu?*"

"I do," he said.

They walked back to the park, and they said their goodbyes.

TWENTY-ONE

A FTER having seen Pierre the first day and Jean-Louis yesterday, today was the day to see Claude. They would meet at five by the statue of Danton at the Odeon. He got there a little early, only to find that Claude had done the same. They both laughed.

"*Bonjour*," he said.

"*Bonjour*," Claude said. They shook hands.

"Follow me," Claude said. They walked to a nearby bar.

Inside, Claude ordered a drink, and he ordered sparkling water.

"Your book is very good," Claude said. "Thank you for your chapter on my work."

"You're welcome. Thank you for taking the time to read it and offer me feedback." They talked about the book for a while, then about Claude's work.

"Where are you currently?"

"Texas," he said.

"You know, the university down in Australia is looking for postdocs. You should apply. You would have to publish a couple analytic things, but that would be easy. I'll talk to Robyn, and see what I can do. We are planning to put on a conference about Kierkegaard. You may be interested," he said.

"That does sound interesting," he said.

There was a pause.

Claude looked at him, "What do you think phenomenology is?"

"The attempt to render intelligible, through description, the essential structures and features of the human condition."

"Pretty good," Claude laughed.

He paused. "Have you read Jean-Louis' new book?"

"I have," he said.

"You know, I was his student," Claude said.

"I didn't know that," he said.

"What about his work? You consider it phenomenological?"

"I think so."

"Even the new one?"

"Yes," he said. He could tell Claude was not convinced.

"He quotes lots of others. I see what he's doing. But I'm not sure it's phenomenology," Claude explained. He wondered whether there might just be a fundamental disagreement that couldn't be resolved on neutral terms. Jean-Louis was a devout believer in Christ, Claude was not. Claude knew he, like Jean-Louis, was a Christian. Maybe Claude was looking for insight into what exactly Jean-Louis and he thought they saw, that Claude hadn't yet.

They finished their drinks and walked back to the Odeon.

"I hope you have a good rest of your trip," he said. "I will be happy to endorse the book. Have your editor get in touch."

"Thank you, that would be wonderful. I'm hoping the rest of the trip goes well. I have so much I want to see with my wife, but I'm busy. Tomorrow I'm going to see Victor for tea, my first day I saw Pierre, and yesterday I saw Jean-Louis."

Claude's jaw dropped in disbelief. "You met Jean-Louis?" Claude had the look of a man who'd just met a thief who'd pulled off what everyone had thought was the impossible heist.

"Yes," he said.

"But how? Jean-Louis very rarely sees anyone," he said.

"He wrote to me, and I told him I was coming to Paris. We talked about the book and other things."

Claude smiled. "Very good," he said. They stared deeply into each other's eyes for a few seconds, then laughed, before turning away and going their separate ways. It was good. Nothing was said, because nothing had to be. They had an agreement.

The next afternoon, it was time for tea at Victor's. The philosopher lived in a slightly different part of the city, not too far from the Champs-Élysées. He took the metro, got off the stop, only got slightly lost, and showed up precisely at four. He rang the buzzer.

"Come up," the voice said.

He walked up the stairs. On the landing, he saw a hand holding the door open. It was Victor.

"Welcome," the man said.

"Hello, thank you," he said.

Victor offered him a chair in the living room. There was an exquisite book shelf, full of many, many volumes, Aristotle, Plato, Husserl, Heidegger, and much else.

"Tea?"

"Yes, please," he said.

For most of the visit, they sat in silence, as Victor stared at the ceiling smoking his pipe. Others he knew had said a visit to Victor's could be awkward, and he now saw why they would say that, but he didn't feel uncomfortable at all. As far as he could tell, they misunderstood Victor. Victor understood the value of silence, whereas they didn't. They took silence as rudeness or disapproval.

Victor looked at him, "So, you are in Texas?"

"Yes."

"At the university?"

"No, at the library."

Victor glanced at him, puffed his pipe, and looked up at the ceiling. "Ah, I see." What he saw, of course, was exactly what nearly everyone else he knew back home pretended not to see, that he was unemployed, and that it made no sense.

They chatted for a while longer, and then he knew it was time to go. He didn't want to overstay his welcome.

"Tell your editor to be in touch," he said.

"I will," he said. "Thank you."

Victor held the door, he walked out, and went down the stairs. Out on the street, he took a deep breath. With their help, this book just may well actually see the light of day, after all, he thought.

TWENTY-TWO

T HE moment he opened the door to the place, he was greeted with a question.

"How'd it go? Tell me everything."

"It was amazing," he said.

"Good. Yesterday when you were meeting with Claude, this feeling of joy and peace overtook me, and I just knew everything was working. I felt the same way today when you were meeting with Victor."

"What's he like?"

"I see why the others say he's eccentric. They say he's awkward, but I didn't find it awkward. He's just quiet. Nobody can stand silence anymore, so they get uncomfortable."

"What did you talk about?"

"The book. Heidegger. Angels. All kinds of things."

"Angels?"

"Yeah."

"Is he going to endorse the book?"

"Yep!"

"Wow, so you're three for three."

"Yeah. Speaking of which, I'm going to email the publisher now." He sat down at the table and wrote a short email to the editor, updating the publisher that he was here in Paris, that he'd met with Jean-Louis, Pierre, Claude, and Victor, and that, in addition to each of them having read the respective chapter on his work, they were waiting for instructions about how to submit their endorsements. He sent it.

"There, that should do it," he said. He did not say explicitly that the editor had been caught lying for saying he'd contact the Frenchmen when he had not. The point was to move on, and to dictate the terms. By already talking about the Frenchman being ready to endorse the book, he was saying that whatever stupid review the publisher was undertaking was pointless. The philosophers themselves had now spoken, some random anonymous reviewers his publisher dug up no longer mattered. Quiller, Klaus, and Carrell would have to learn to live with it.

TWENTY-THREE

I T was the day after returning from Paris, Friday. Alison was at work, and things were as before. He was at his desk again, only now there wasn't anything to write. The book was done, and he was simply waiting to hear something, anything, from the publisher. The email he'd been awaiting arrived. He read it carefully. The editor wrote to confirm that he'd been in touch with the Frenchman, who had confirmed that they were indeed thrilled to endorse the book. When he had the endorsements, the editor would be in touch, to begin the production process. A few hours later, Billy Luce, whom he had not heard from in quite a while, wrote as well. He had three anonymous reviews. Two were positive. The third was highly critical. Judging by the review's tone and style, it came from whom he'd expect it to have come from. Philosophically, there was nothing he wasn't anticipating. He drafted a long and thorough response, sent it off, and went outside to his chair. He'd enjoy the rest of the day when everyone else came to terms with the fact that there was no stopping the book.

The next day, Luce was back. He was satisfied with the response. Publication was confirmed, although still no date was set. There should by now have been talk about marketing and galleys, but he'd long ago written off the standard niceties of academic publishing. His only goal was to get the book to appear. If it did, that would be a success. Shortly after receiving the note from Luce, he received another follow-up note from the other editor, confirming a detail about the book cover. "Have a good weekend," it said. Odd, he thought. The note was out of character for his editor.

That evening, he went for a walk. He called his dad.

"Hello?"

"It's me."

"How's it going?"

"Good," he said.

They talked about where things stood. A block from home, some-body came from behind and hit him in the back of the head. He nearly fell to the ground, but he kept his footing. Somebody hit him again. Then again. There were two attackers. He dropped the phone and spun around. Two young men were on him, punching him and trying to restrain his arms. They wrangled him against a car where they kept hitting him. He began crying for help, but it was late, and his attackers had waited to jump him in front of an abandoned property. Soon his chest was heaving, and he was out of breath. He couldn't cry out. He felt one of his attackers re-lease his arm, as the man reached for something in his pocket. It might be a knife. He turned around with what was left of his strength and faced his two attackers. Their eyes were as wide as saucers. Evidently, they couldn't believe he was still standing. Neither could he. They ran.

He looked into the street where he saw a white sedan had been idling. He walked over to the driver side. The man had the window down.

"Did you see that?"

The man was stunned. He nodded his head.

"Could you call the police?"

The man was silent.

"Call the police!"

The car sped off. It dawned on him. The man in the car had been the getaway driver. The two men who had jumped him had meant to put him in the car. When he didn't get knocked out or go down, they had ended up struggling with him longer than they had bargained for, the getaway driver hadn't known what to do, and when he saw the attackers run, he had frozen. He walked to the sidewalk looking for his things. When they had him pinned up against the car, they'd pulled out his wallet and thrown it on the ground.

He called the police. A few minutes later, a car arrived.

The two cops took out their flashlights. "You the victim?"

"Yes."

"You know which way they ran off?"

He pointed toward Midtown.

"You know them?"

"No."

"They take anything?"

"No. They threw everything on the ground." The cops looked at each other.

"Where?"

"Over there," he said pointing. The cops looked with their flashlights for a few minutes. They found the headset for his phone, which had been knocked off his head from the initial strike.

"This yours?"

"Yeah, that flew off from the punch."

"You sure they didn't take anything?"

"Yeah."

"What about your shoes?"

He laughed. He'd forgotten he was barefoot. "No, they didn't take my shoes. I live on the other side of the block. I was outside my apartment talking to my dad, and I decided to take a short walk."

"Okay, I see." The cops talked to one other quietly for a minute, then came to him.

"Here's the number to call."

"Homicide?"

"Yeah, homicide. This wasn't a robbery. They didn't take anything. You were targeted. Call the homicide guys and tell them what you know before anyone transfers it over to assault." They got in the car and drove off.

He laughed to himself and shook his head as he walked home. All things considered, this was a good weekend, after all. Somebody apparently had tried to abduct him, but he was still here. He had a good idea of who was behind it, but at this point it didn't matter. The book would be out soon, and nobody could stop it.

Over the coming weeks, the endorsements, which were all stellar, arrived. The Frenchmen, who were very smart, sent them directly to him, after which he would send them on to the editor. The editor couldn't complain, since at this point the caution was reasonable. There was no reason to allow the publisher to "miss" an endorsement. They put up a bit a bit of a struggle over Claude's. Shortly after he sent it, his editor replied saying how wonderful the endorsement was, which is what made it all the more terrible for him to have to say that it would be too late to use it on the book jacket. When he pointed out that the publisher still hadn't even set a publication date, and that he as the author was personally willing to delay production for as long as it was necessary to include Claude's endorsement, the publisher waved the towel, changed its mind, and said that it would be possible to use the endorsement, after all. He was fine if Quiller and Klaus fought him tooth and nail to the very end. He'd expected it.

What he hadn't expected was the development that came later that summer. It was July, the academic term was about to begin, and he had resigned himself to another year in Texas, without a position somewhere. Then, out of the blue, Vanderbilt contacted him. He'd submitted an application last fall there for an assistant professorship. Someone else had gotten it. He hadn't received an interview. They had a postdoc, however, and they wanted to know whether he was interested. The timing was suspicious, and something felt synthetic about it, but at this point, he wasn't going to be picky. Besides, Alison would be overjoyed. He accepted an interview, which was set for the day after next. His suspicions only intensified, when instead of the usual selection committee, only the chair and assistant chair were present to interview him. But again, he figured he'd play along. A couple weeks later, they offered him the job, he accepted, and signed the paperwork. Out of nowhere, Alison and he would be off to Nashville.

When the paperwork had been finalized, he had forwarded news of the job to Linda and Stuart. They remained silent. So, too, did most of the rest of his family. After two years of everyone playing along with the story that he was a delusional misfit with no academic future, the fact that his book was about to appear and that he'd landed a post at Vanderbilt didn't fit the story. In response, everyone did what he knew they would do. They ignored the good news.

In just a few days, he would drive to Nashville with Myskin and Umi. Alison, who was finishing her final two weeks at work, would be close behind, flying a few days after him. They would get a hotel in town, while they looked for a place. Time was short, because in just two weeks, the term would start. He would be teaching classes he'd not taught before, but he was confident he could teach them well enough, since he'd read fairly extensively in the relevant areas at Oxford. Good teaching, anyway, was mostly about commitment. And he was committed.

He took what would be one of his final walks through the neighborhood. On campus, he bumped into an old professor of his, Chuck Brown. Chuck was in his late fifties, a man whose haunted face revealed the weight of years of sin. He was divorced, and the ensuing years of serial monogamy had not done him any favors. At one time, they had more or less been sympatico, but now, as their respective allegiances to the flesh and Spirit had only intensified, the divergence between them was wider than ever. Stay on the path he had been on before, and in twenty or so years he would be right where Chuck was now. It was a sobering reminder of what not to become. He could see Chuck was not expecting to encounter him.

"Hi, Chuck," he said.

"Oh, uh, hi," Chuck said. He understood Chuck's alarm. In addition to being a colleague of Carrell, the frazzled professor was close friends with Klaus and Dowell.

Chuck fumbled for words. "What are you doing here?"

"Just out for a walk. Figured I'd enjoy the beautiful campus here one last time. Alison and I are moving to Nashville. I landed a postdoc."

"Oh, congratulations," Chuck said.

"Thanks," he said. "The book should be out soon."

Chuck's eyes widened, and before he could stop himself, he'd said too much, "But, what about the review?"

He smiled. He had never once said a word to Chuck about the state of the book manuscript. The only way Chuck could have known about the review, then, is if Carrell, or Klaus, or Dowell had mentioned it. Nobody evidently had bothered to tell Chuck that the original plan to sink the manuscript in review had failed. As a result, Chuck had still been under the impression that the book was never coming out, and that the publisher would be able to block it as Oxford had tried with the dissertation.

"The review? Oh, I took care of that already," he said.

Discombobulated, Chuck stared into space, as it sunk in with him that somebody hadn't kept him apprised. "Oh," he said.

"Take care, Chuck," he said walking away.

He left campus and walked through the surrounding streets. After two years, it was hard to believe they were finally leaving. Strangely, he was going to miss it. The book hadn't yet been released, and he still didn't even have a publication date from the publisher. He had accepted things for what they were. There would be no marketing. There would be no book launch. There wouldn't even be galleys. None of that mattered. It would be a colossal accomplishment simply to see it appear at all.

He walked into the neighborhood used book store. Though he did not know it yet standing where he was, a few months later, after the book had finally been released, the Provost of Vanderbilt would note the bizarreness of the situation. It would be an encounter he would not forget. The author copies had arrived late, of course. And there was a terrible printing error that left an ugly black mark down the page. But he wouldn't care. That all could be fixed later. The publisher had suddenly rushed it to print, having never expected to ever have to print it.

In the office, the Provost held a copy of the mangled book up in his hand. In a French accent, the man said one word that said it all, "*Miracle.*"

His attention returned to the books around him. He perused the shelves. For years, he'd been meaning to read Rousseau. He took a copy of *First and Second Discourses*. He was about to select some more books, when the phone rang.

"Are you still at the bookstore?"

"Yeah." Alison sounded upset.

"Can I come get you there?"

"Sure, I'll wait outside."

A few minutes later, the car pulled up and he got inside. Alison was crying.

"What's wrong?"

"My parents. I just came from their house. I just spent the afternoon arguing with them."

"About what?"

"About you and Oxford."

"What?"

"Yeah, I told them that you're leaving for the job at Vanderbilt, and that my dad still hasn't talked to you about anything's that happened. He's still refusing to talk," she said.

He sighed. "Do you want me to go back over there with you?"

She nodded tearfully, "Yes."

"Do you want me to drive?"

"No, I can drive."

"Okay, let's go."

"Promise me you won't get mad."

"Promise."

"There's something else."

"What?"

"You got an email from Dave's wife. There's been a road accident, and he's in a coma." He shook his head incredulously. First the Oxford Proctor, and now his former London solicitor.

"It's my fault," he said solemnly.

"Don't feel guilty. It's not your fault," she said.

When they got to the house, Alison knocked. No answer. She knocked again. A few moments later, they saw Linda and Stuart coming to the door.

Linda opened the door with a look of feigned bewilderment on her face. "Hi, honey, we weren't expecting to see you tonight. Is everything okay?" Stuart stood behind his wife silently.

"Mom, we have to talk. I've been begging you for two years to talk about what's going on. Why won't you talk about it?"

"Honey, you need to calm down," Linda said.

"I am calm," Alison said. She turned to him, "He's been followed and attacked three times. The Proctor is dead in a car accident. Now the lawyer is in a coma from a road accident. Something's going on, and you and Dad need to talk to us about it."

Stuart spoke, "We are cooking dinner right now. This is a bad time. We will have to do this another time," he said.

"What? We can't come in?" Alison said.

"We will do this another time," Stuart said again.

"When? We're about to leave for Nashville."

"How about tomorrow?" Linda said.

"Fine."

"Where do you want to meet?"

Alison looked at him. "Where should we do it?" He thought about it. Campus would be perfect. Right where Carrell liked to meet his students. Right where all of Stuart's colleagues and students were. "How about the campus coffee shop?"

Alison turned to Linda, "Let's meet there."

Linda shook her head, "No, no that won't work."

He decided it was time to step in. "Why not, Linda? You just said Alison should choose the place. And what, you shoot down her very first suggestion? Why?"

"Stop arguing. You're being very aggressive," Stuart said.

"I'm not being aggressive. I'm just asking a simple question," he said.

"Linda said she doesn't want to meet at campus. Pick another place," Stuart said.

"Your daughter asks for bread, and you give her a stone. Unbelievable," he said.

Alison was crying. He put his hand on her back and turned to her, "Come on, Barnacle, I'm sorry, this is a waste of time." She took his hand, as he faced Linda and Stuart. "Enjoy your dinner," he said.

They got in the car and drove home. There was nothing to say, so they both said nothing.

Twenty-four

A FEW weeks later, they had found a place in Nashville, and moved in all of their things. It wasn't yet home, but eventually it would be. They lied down on the bed, the moving boxes stacked up in the hall.

"I love you," he said.

"I don't know," she said.

"What do you mean?"

"I don't know if you really do," she said.

"Of course, I love you," he said.

She looked down and shook her head gently, then she looked at him. "Do you think what it says is true?"

He knew exactly what she was talking about.

"Yes," he said.

"How did you know what I meant?"

"I know you," he said.

"So, you do think it's true?"

"Yes," he said.

"I hope not. I want to be with you forever. I want us to be together," she said.

"You will. We will," he said.

"But not like that. I want to be your wife," she said.

He was quiet.

She looked at him. "If that's what being like an angel is, I don't want to be one. Human is fine," she said. He was quiet.

"Do you regret it?"

"No," he said.

"You don't regret marrying me?"

"No," he said. "Sometimes I think you regret it."

"I don't," she said.

He was quiet.

"I just wish we could go back," she said.

As she spoke, he was already reaching to put on an old song he had not played in some time, one that reminded him of their engagement, because it had almost been their wedding song. She recognized the opening chords from the acoustic guitar instantaneously, and before the singer could finish the first lines of the song, there were tears trickling down her cheeks. She closed her eyes and put her head on his chest.

> So many lives were lived out today.
> At times felt like my chances were slipping away.
> The window is open, if you can just climb on through.
> The truth isn't always spoken, just something you do,
> Something you do.

The song's melody began saturating the room.

> Smelled summer on the breath of the city tonight.
> Watched the sky fade to blue and pink,
> And thought I only get one life.
> My feet fractured the sidewalks,
> The years piled high.

Anticipating the coming lines, his consciousness was led to constitute the night he had met his friend visiting from Texas at the bus stop outside Tom Gate. He hadn't known it, but other than Alison, it would be his only visitor that first year in Oxford. His friend had stepped off the bus into the night, the fog enveloping them both, and looked up at the streetlamps. "I've only just arrived, and it's already lonely here. I don't know how you do it," his friend had said standing in the mist. At his desk, they'd opened the window and smoked cigarettes together. When he had put on the song, his friend had tapped his knee and nodded his head as he hummed along to the melody. "Interesting, it's a waltz."

> I stood under this streetlamp,
> Asked myself the same questions too many times,
> Too many times.

Here in the room, the melody crested, then crashed, then unfolded all over once again, as Alison began drying her tears with his white shirt.

There was a thud from something landing on the bed, then a loud meow. Then another. "Myshkie, come here, little blind man," Alison said, pulling him in. She laughed softly as the cat nuzzled his face against hers. "He's a good little man," she said petting him.

The song continued,

> Hope you'll love me the same way,
> When the colors are grey on grey.

> Hope you'll love me the same way.

> Hope you'll love me the same way,
> When the colors are grey on grey.

> Hope you'll love me the same way,
> The same way.

The music stopped, but the melody lingered. The visible room looked empty, but they both could feel that it wasn't.

"I love you."